The Gas Attendant

ISBN: 1-4196-6102-7
ISBN-13: 9781419661020

The Gas Attendant

Rick Naylor

Dedication

LUKE and LUDIE...

Growing up as one of your eight children was a treat. You made us laugh, even through the tough times. DAD the stories that you told always made us smile and sometimes had us laughing hysterically. MOM the quilts that you weaved, kept us warm on those cold southern nights and the meals that you prepared, even when the cupboard was bare, filled our stomach and heart with joy. WE HAD FUN!

Things seem so much easier today, than they were for us back then. You both taught us how important family was at an early age. I have tried to instill the things that you taught me in my four kids, Brandon, Brittany, Kimberly, Derrick and I think they got it.

Mom and Dad; you both left us much too soon as did our siblings (Bubba) Luke Jr., Darryl and recently the youngest of us all…Sandra. Even my nephew Mario left us too soon. It is my hope that you are all up in heaven looking down on us with smiles on your faces. I hope that you don't see everything that we do LOL…but I hope you see all the good things that we do. Please take comfort in the fact that you raised all your kids well. We love and miss you all so much! Rest in Peace.

Content

Characters

Prologue

The little antique gas station on the corner of 19th and Clover located on the Eastside of Long Island, New York had always been known as a place of mystery since the owner found his wife and her German lover dead on the back seat of his 56 Chevy on Christmas Eve in 1957. Apparently, they had fallen asleep after making love and left the car running in the enclosed garage.

This is the official police finding however, the people in the neighborhood think they were killed by the "spirit" of the gas attendant. His name was Aubrey and he also died in the garage a few weeks earlier when the car he was working on fell on top of him.

He was also found by the owner.

The people in the neighborhood are certain that the place is haunted. They attempt to burn it down on New Year's Eve of that same year. Their efforts are unsuccessful. It is rumored that the gas attendant would not allow them to carry out their arsenic plan. This setback only made the people in the neighborhood more suspicious of the place. How could the gas attendant stop them? He was dead…

Now fifty years later the past is about to reveal a dark secret that no one on the island is prepared to handle. The garage is also ready to claim its next victim.

Will it succeed or will someone finally figure out the key to this mystery and send the ghostly spirit to its final resting place?

Introduction

The shocked crowd stood one block away watching in awe as the firemen frantically raced around trying to extinguish the flames.

Some knew this day would come but most wished that it never would. The old gas station had been a fixture in the neighborhood for over seventy years. Everyone hoped that the firemen could save the place but their efforts seemed useless.

A stranger standing under an oak tree two blocks away smiled as the flames grew higher. She only wished that she had the courage to set it on fire herself. The stranger pulled the cap down over her long auburn hair and adjusted her glasses. She was dressed in jeans that were three sizes too big for her small body. If she looked at herself in a mirror, she would not recognize herself. She was sure no one from her old home town would know her. It was time to make her move. She exhaled and headed for the flaming building.

Someone yelled, "the gas attendant is still in the building!" The firemen rushed in and found him unconscious lying on the floor. In his hand was a picture and a twenty dollar bill. Although he was indeed unconscious; his grip on these two items were firm.

As they were putting the gas attendant into the ambulance, the stranger ran up to him and attempted to pry the picture from his hand but she was unsuccessful. Two bystanders wrestled her away from the ambulance but not before she got a good look at the man inside. He was barely breathing and she knew he would be dead soon. She had seen death many times.

Seeing him like that saddened her a little but she wanted that picture. She had to have it! She had to get away from this horrible, horrible place before someone recognized her.

As she watched the ambulance roll away, the lights had a hypnotic effect on her. The trance was broken when she heard a familiar voice calling her name. It was a name that she hadn't heard in over 30 years. The deep haunting voice was unmistakable and it sent shivers down her spine. How had he recognized her?

She wanted to run but she knew it would do no good. The inhuman thing with the battered face that was calling her name would not allow it. So she bravely turned to face her past and the torment that surely awaited her...

Chapter 1

Rich removed his wet boots and tossed them in the corner to dry. It was just another ordinary boring night in a town called Hempstead, New York.

After locating the old electric heater and cautiously plugging it into the wall. He prepared himself for a spark but there was no spark this time. What a relief, he thought.

Careful placement of the heater was important. Too close and the heat would burn a hole in his precious boots. Too far away and the heat wouldn't dry them quickly enough.

Three weeks ago, he burned a hole in the left boot near the bottom. He had placed a carefully crafted piece of cardboard in the boot since and that worked pretty well; except on the days that it rained. Normally, this delicate drying process took about an hour, if the old heater didn't trip the circuit breaker, which had to be reset a thousand times. Something really needed to be done about the wiring in this old place. These were his only shoes. If he were lucky there would be no customers before they dried. Unfortunately, luck was never on his side. Two more customers came within the next ten minutes. Putting the wet boots back on was very uncomfortable…

Rich was six feet, five inches tall and weighed a modest two hundred pounds. He had really been a "ladies man" in his home town of Northport, South Carolina but he really didn't miss those days. Life just seemed simpler without all the hassle that a relationship would bring. However, there were nights when all he could think about was a woman like Karen Vonhart and her insatiable sexual desires. That skinny woman really knew how to make love to a man.

Rich stared out the dirty rain soaked window of the gas station. What a dark, wet and dreary night this has turned out to be. The raindrops are the size of fifty-cent pieces and when they hit you, the sting seemly lasts forever.

When he was a kid he accidentally wondered into a hornet's nest at his grandfather's farm back in South Carolina. He remembered the sting of those bites to be similar to the gigantic rain spears that cascaded from the sky tonight.

His last customer was over an hour ago but he could still feel the pain as the deluge of rain slapped against his now redden, prickly face as the elderly customer said, "filler up son".

The pumps at the station were old and slower than a snail crossing a turtle's path. If that wasn't bad enough, throw in the fact that there was no shelter over them. This only added to the misery of working at this "marvelous place".

It's been raining four days straight now with no signs of letting up. Rich was a fan of Greek Mythology and wondered briefly if the Gods were irritated and sent the rain spears to punish those silly enough to be out in this weather. No he thought, they had better things to do with their time, at least he hoped...

The rain always brought back so many memories to him. When he was young, it seemed that every time it rained, his father would have this big silly smile on his face and tell his mother that it was "baby making weather". When he asked his father what that meant, he would laugh and reply that he was too young to understand. When he asked his mother, her pale white cheeks would suddenly turn redder than an apple. She would pat him on his head and say go play.

Rich was almost nineteen before he understood what that phrase meant. Thanks mostly to a prostitute named Luanne on a rainy night in Georgia, on a hard bed in a cheap motel located on a famous strip nicknamed "Victory Drive" in a town called Columbus. That was where many of the mighty soldiers of Fort Benning, Georgia either got lucky or got an S.T.D. Sometimes the ladies of the night served up both.

It was on this famous strip that Rich was well educated in all the ways of baby making. The first thing that he did after the voluminously, beautiful Asian whore took his virginity was call his father and inform him that he completely understood what "baby making weather" was all about. His father laughed for over an hour.

Rich was sadden to learn that two weeks later the beautiful prostitute that had taken his virginity like a thief on Christmas Eve was found beaten and left for dead. Apparently some angry G.I. had fallen in love with her and was distrait when she made it known that the only thing that she loved was his money.

"Did Arnold over sleep again?" he wondered.

It had been such a long day and Rich was so tired, all he wanted to do was go to his tiny one room apartment and crawl onto his tiny sofa sleeper with the hard mattress and sleep until it was time to come back to this "wonderful place."

This was not the life that he had envisioned when he hitched his prized 1982 Porsche 924 to a Uhaul truck packed with his art and headed to the Big Apple.

Unfortunately, the beautiful old car that saved the Porsche Company from going bankrupt didn't fare well after just two weeks of the "big potholes" in the "Big Apple" but it had been nice that first week cruising down Manhattan as the locals checked out the beautiful little Porsche. It was also nice to check out the women. There were millions of them and they all needed a man. Everything was so new then and New York still was a city to be explored for all its glory...now it was just good to get home safely every night.

Not having a car makes nights like this even worse for Rich. All of the buses had stopped running and catching a taxi was simply out of the question.

"Where is Arnold?" thought Rich. *He was always tardy but tonight he was extremely late to the tune of three hours.*

"I'm trying not to get upset because I like you...but if I were Mr. Sanford, I would have fired your tardy ass a long, long time ago. Where are you old man?" screamed Rich.

Rich knew the truth of the matter was Arnold was the life's blood of this place. Without him the station would probably have gone under years ago. Rich and Mr. Sanford both knew it. So he was sure that Mr. Sanford was probably just joking about firing the old guy besides, Arnold had been here almost twenty years. Unofficially, they were partners and Mr. Sanford knew it.

Unlike Arnold, Rich had no plans of spending the rest of his life in this dump. The pay is terrible and so are the hours. Arnold and he manned the place 24 hours a day, seven days a week, just the two of them.

The only time they closed was half day on Thanksgiving. It was Rich's favorite holiday since moving to New York because that was the day when Mr. Sanford would invite them to his home for dinner. There would be a feast and the food tasted great. There was always enough food left over to take some home and the leftovers would last for days.

On Christmas the place was open as usual. According to Mr. Sanford, it was a business decision and strangely the station's most profitable day of the year. For some reason the boss didn't celebrate Christmas, he didn't appear to be an atheist but not celebrating this day was strange to Rich.

The old station was built back in the mid fifties when they built things to last but it needed a lot of TLC. However, there was never any sign that the boss would fix up the place. The station still had nineteen fifties gas pumps for goodness sake.

Mr. Sanford liked it that way. He said it gave the place character. I'm not knocking the place Rich had thought on many occasions because it's more than he had but he was sure that he would have done something about those ugly gas pumps. Besides, who in their right mind would buy gas at a place that had pumps like these?

When Rich started working here two years ago, this job was a gift from God. He was so broke he couldn't pay attention. He never thought he'd still be here two years later. A few weeks, maybe a month he thought. Boy did he miss the call on that one.

Like most people who were brave or stupid enough to leave the comforts of home, he also came to New York with big dreams. He was an artist back then, "probably believes he still is". Anyway, his plans were to sell his art and move into one of those fancy, high rise penthouse apartments with a magnificent view of the Hudson River on the East Side of Manhattan.

Nobody warned him how expensive or competitive the "Big Apple" could be. His first week here, the poor guy showed his art to anyone and everyone. Most people were nice and complimented him but no one offered him one red cent for any of them.

With funds and patience running short after just one week, he found himself moving to a less than desirable neighborhood east of New York City.

His dream high rise luxury penthouse turned out to be a one room apartment that was only two stories high with no view of anything." As bad as things appeared, it wasn't as bad as high tailing it back home to Carolina.

A voice in his head told him a hundred times that he should have listened to his girlfriend. Her name was Karen and they had dated for five years before he moved to the East Coast.

He knew she thought he was an idiot, "with idiot dreams." She never came out and said it but sometimes a look can be worth a thousand words. Everyone knows the, "you are an idiot look" and she gave it to him on several occasions just prior to his move here.

Karen dumped him after his second month in the Big Apple. The Dear John letter simple said, "he was too much of a dreamer, Grow Up".

Three weeks later she moved in with a guy named Elroy Johnston and shortly there after married the guy. Everything was fine the first week until Elroy's wife followed him one night and found him shacked up with his skinny new bride.

Lydia Johnston was a large woman with man like hands and arms. She didn't think her husband of fifteen years being married to another woman was such a great idea. Before calling the police she beat Elroy with a green rubber garden hose until he bled "hillbilly blue" as he shamelessly begged for mercy in front of his new bride. The begging did him no good because Lydia wasn't listening.

Once her arms grew tired of beating him, she took her "sawed off shot gun," placed it in Mr. Elroy's mouth and demanded that he climb on top of his new wife and have sex with her. The expression on Elroy and Karen's face was priceless. Fear was emanate and they both knew the Grim Reaper might be making an appearance tonight.

Poor Elroy was so terrified that he wasn't able to get it up. He had always dreamed of being with two women at the same time but not like this...no not like this. Lydia grew tired of waiting for him to get his limp penis up. *It was a situation that she was very familiar with.*

She was furious with her man and made him sit in a chair and watch as she tied his skinny new wife to the bed post. Although this woman was some what of a runt, she could see why her unfaithful husband could be attracted to those, "juicy peach size breasts".

Lydia called her brother Pete, her cousins Sam and Kenny Ray to come see her unfaithful husband's new wife. When they got there, they were also impressed with the skinny woman's beautiful breasts, with the hard one inch nipples. It appeared that all the attention was arousing the skinny woman but that could not be farther from the truth.

An hour after everyone had touched and groped the skinny woman Lydia finally called the Sheriff.

When the Sheriff arrived, poor Karen had urinated on herself twice and had cried a river of tears. She tried to explain to Lydia that she didn't know Elroy was married but it did no good. *"Lydia wasn't listening."*

Lydia told her brother Justin who had been the Sheriff for less than two months to lock Elroy away for a long time. Her brother did the next best thing...

He released Karen and told her that they were giving her a twenty minute head start. He informed her that when they caught her, they would rip her body to pieces like a pack of hungry wolves on an antelope. He opened the door and said, *"get gone"*...

Karen ran through the dark snow covered woods falling several times not knowing where she was going. She heard Elroy scream twice and could only imagine what they had just done to him. A part of her was happy but another part, the part that wanted to live, "ran like Satan was tugging on her skirt with his pitch fork."

A few minutes later she heard a gunshot. At first she feared that Elroy had met his end by gunshot but then there was another shot and a branch flew off a tree just a few feet in front of her. She glanced at her watch. Twenty minutes had passed quickly. Oh my God! She heard herself scream, "they are shooting at me..."

Rich often wondered if this story told to him by a close friend was true. The only one that could truly confirm it for him was Karen but he didn't expect that he'd be hearing from her any time soon.

The one thing that he was certain of is Karen now knows that he's not the only idiot from Northport, South Carolina.

"Where is Arnold?" thought Rich. I have to get some sleep. If I'm here another two hours, I might as well stay here. It wouldn't be the first time that I had stayed over but Mr. Sanford made it clear that he didn't approve. I should call him and let him know about Arnold. Maybe he'll let me close the station until Arnold gets here.

"Hello...

"Mr. Arnold...I'm sorry to be calling you so late but Arnold is not here yet."

"That damn Arnold! I'm going to fire him. I'll give him a call and see what the problem is. Oh wait...I can't call him, he doesn't have a phone. Go ahead and close up Rich; you must be exhausted. I'll ride over to his place. He might be feeling under the weather, if so, I'll come in myself for a few hours. He's never been this late. He probably just over slept again."

"Who was that on the phone Harold?"

"Don't worry about it, just go back to sleep. I have to go to the station. Arnold is late again."

"Why don't you fire his old, slow butt!?"

"Go back to sleep woman and let me handle my own affairs! However, if you feel that you must meddle in my business, get your old ass dressed and come with me. I could probably use the company."

"You're a crazy old man. Thanks but no thanks; I think I will let you handle your own business at 2:00a.m. on this freezing cold morning.

"Fine you old witch, just stay there and keep my bed warm until I get back.

It seemed as though I had only closed my eyes for about two seconds, when I was awaken by a loud noise. Someone was beating on the door like there was a fire.

It must be Arnold finally but just in case, I cautiously made my way to the front door. I noticed bright lights gleaming through the filthy windows of the ancient gas station, so I hurried my pace a bit. The lights were from a police car. I slowly opened the door and addressed the short officer. He wore his hat tilted slightly to one side so that his huge glasses didn't get in the way. His shoes were spotless; the shine from them almost matched the glaring lights from his brand new cruiser.

"Hello, may I help you?" said Rich.

"I'm sorry to disturb you; my name is Sergeant Malloy."

"How can I help you Sergeant?"

"I'm afraid that I have some bad news."

"Oh my, I was afraid of that. It's Arnold isn't it?"

"Who is Arnold?"

"He's my relief; he was supposed to be here five hours ago."

"Sorry fellow, that name doesn't ring a bell. I'm here about Mr. Harold Sanford. He is the proprietor of this fine establishment isn't he?"

Huh…"yes he is."

"I'm afraid that he has been in a terrible accident."

"Oh no…is he ok?"

"He's at West Side General right now, I'm afraid it doesn't look good. He's in a coma. Apparently, he fell asleep while driving and hit a utility pole."

"Oh no, this is my fault. I should have never called him about Arnold."

"Do you know how we can reach his family?"

"Sergeant, as far as I know…he only has one daughter and they haven't spoken in years. She lives somewhere in Tennessee and I'm afraid that I don't know how to contact her. Arnold has worked here over twenty years; maybe he knows how to reach her".

"Well now…Arnold isn't here. Is he Richie? When do you expect him to get here?"

"Like I said earlier Sergeant; he should have been here five hours ago. He works the graveyard shift. He normally makes it in around 11:00pm or shortly there after."

"Does he live close?"

"Yes, about nine maybe ten blocks."

"Describe him to me."

"He's in his early fifties, skinny fellow, weighs about a buck fifty soaking wet."

"Richie does he have a tattoo on the left side of his neck?"

"Yes…as a matter of fact he does. Sergeant, how you know that?"

"I'm the law son. It's my job to know things. Excuse me for a minute Richie. I'll be right back."

Rich watched the short but proud little policeman walk quickly but awkwardly to his cruiser. The Sergeant had a noticeable limp. In less than two minutes he was headed back toward the station with a grim expression on his face. Rich tried to brace himself for the news…

"Well Richie...I'm afraid that I know why your friend Arnold didn't make it to work last night. The description that you just gave me is a perfect match for a John Doe that was found around midnight, less than six blocks from here. Looks like robbery."

"Dear God officer (sob) please tell me that you are mistaken. The poor guy doesn't have a cent to his name. Anyone could just look at him and see that. He's (sob) always broke, just like me. All his money is spent on rent and tomorrow is payday, so I'm sure he was broke."

"I'm sorry Rich; I know this must be hard on you. There is one sure way to find out if it's Arnold. Lets take a trip to the morgue and see if it's your friend."

"Wait a minute Sergeant. This is a lot to take in at the moment. Can you give me a few minutes to get myself together?"

"I'll wait for you in the car Richie. Do you have anything to drink in there?"

"We have soda pop. Will that do?"

"Sure...do you have a grape one?"

"I think so. Yep here you go."

"Thank you. I didn't know they still made soda pops in these old bottles. It really takes me back a lot of years. Wow...it even tastes the same."

"I'm glad you like it. I don't care much for the taste myself but my boss insists on buying them. He really believes people prefer these old watered down drinks. If this was my place the first thing I would do is get some real sodas in here."

"That's because you are still a young buck. When I was a kid I would order one of these with two straws."

"Why did you need two straws?"

"One straw was for me and the other for my date."

"That sounds a little cheap to me," said a heart broken Rich.

"It wasn't cheap. It was romantic. At least that's what the girls said. Besides, this place needs a coat of paint far worst than it needs those new carbonated, sugar filled drinks. Let's go Richie. After you I.D. the body, maybe you should go straight to the hospital and see your boss."

"I'd like to do that but I don't have a car and I can't afford a taxi."

"For Christ sake man, this is your boss we're talking about."

"I know but you said West Side General didn't you?"

"Yes I did."

"Well, that's clear across town. A taxi will charge me an arm and two legs to take me there and then I would have to worry about getting back here."

"You really don't have a car?"

"No I don't."

"I'll get a squad car to take you there but I'm afraid you'll be on your own getting back."

"Thanks Sergeant that will be a great help. What a night!"

Rich walked around to the front passenger side of the car but Malloy motioned him to the back seat. Riding in the back of the cruiser felt weird. As if Malloy sensed Rich's unease, he said, "sorry company policy"...the little man punched the accelerator and Rich reached for his seat belt but there wasn't one.

"How long have you worked at this station?"

"April will be two years."

"You're not from around here are you?"

"No, I'm from South Carolina."

"Yes, I thought I detected a southern twang to that voice. You definitely won't be mistaken for a New Yorker."

"Thank you. I will take that as a compliment."

"Ha, ha…did you come all the way to the Big Apple to work at a gas station?"

"No but I don't really feel like talking about it."

"You don't have to explain. I can tell you are one of those dreamers.

"What do you mean?"

"Look Richie, New York is the largest city in these United States but for some reason everyone thinks they can come here and grab a slice of the "Big Apple" for themselves. Well let me tell you fellow…that darn "Apple" isn't big enough for those of us who were born here. So am I right?"

"Yeah, I was chasing a dream."

"What kind of a dream Richie?"

"Please don't call me Richie. It's becoming very irritating. My name is Rich and I'm an artist."

Ok, "I'm sorry." What kind of artist? I mean do you make those little statues or do you draw? We have lots of picture drawers here."

"I'm not a picture drawer. I'm an artist! I was always told my work was good and I still believe it. It's just not good enough to put food on the table, at least not yet. Unfortunately, I haven't sold a single piece of art since I've been here. I haven't even tried in over a year."

"Well who told you to move here and try to sell that stuff in the first place?"

"A lot of people from back home thought it was a good idea."

"I see...so the gas station was plan B...?"

"No Sergeant; the gas station wasn't in the plans at all. I had stopped there because my car had been over heating. Just as I approached the gas station it starting to jerk and then suddenly there was a cloud of white smoke coming out the exhaust. I pulled into the station and the car went dead. I tried to start it several times but with no luck."

"Sounds like you blew a head gasket Rich. What kind of car was it?"

"It was a 1982 Porsche."

"What model?"

"It was the 924 model."

"You got to be kidding me...you were driving that little car in this big city? It's also a slow car. You're lucky someone didn't run over you and flatten you like a pancake. How did you even get into the thing? You look like you're about six feet, seven inches tall."

"That's close Sergeant but I suppose that's part of your job. How much you think I weigh?"

"I'd say about a hundred and eighty pounds. Wait I should add another ten pounds because of that hippie length hair that you have. Have you always worn it in a pony tail?"

"No I haven't, I just started that since I've been here."

"Well, you definitely don't look like a New Yorker either."

"Thanks...but then again neither do half the people that live here." What exactly does a real New Yorker look like? Aside from the accent, I can't really tell. Are you a real New Yorker?"

"Yes, born and raised here asshole and so were my parents and my grandparents. So how did you land the job at the station?

"There was a sign on the door that said help wanted on the day that my car broke down and at that point I definitely needed help. The owner was actually looking for someone with a mechanical background to run the garage. Unfortunately, I don't know much about working on cars but he felt sorry for me and hired me anyway. He even paid to have my car towed to the junkyard, he did however, take the money out of my first check. I only planned to work there for a few weeks. That was almost two years ago. I've looked for other jobs but there was always one issue or another that keep me from taking one."

"I guess it's a good thing your car broke down there."

"Maybe Sergeant but the jury is still out on that one."

"I know you just told me that you don't work on cars but do you have any ideal what that Porsche of yours was worth?"

"No not really. It was a gift from my Grand-father. So as far as I'm concerned that made it priceless. He didn't have much use for it as he got older. He was also constantly making costly repairs on it."

"What shape was the body in?"

"It was in great shape. I had just had it paint-ed a couple of months before I moved here. It was a beautiful car but it wasn't much good to me not running."

"Well running or not Rich, it's worth more than some new cars these days. Are you sure your boss had it towed to the junkyard?"

"That's what he said."

"That's very interesting Rich...

"Why do you say it like that?"

"Well now your boss owns a gas station with a garage, which tells me that he is somewhat of a businessman, which also tells me that he knew the true value of that car. It would have cost less than thirty dollars to have the car towed to the junkyard but it would have cost the same amount to have it towed to a mechanic. If all you had was a blown head gasket, it could have been fixed for around a hundred dollars and someone would have a nice antique Porsche to show off."

"Can we change the subject Sergeant?"

"Sure...tell me about Arnold."

"He was a quiet man, even a little mysterious at times. He loved the Mets and despised the Yankees with a passion. I never really understood that. Most people I've met here either love one or the other but not both. Why not root for both teams?"

"Man with that kind of an attitude I can see why you haven't sold any painting. This is a city divided, Richie my boy. It's the East against the West. It's the North against the South. The city is huge but there is only room to root for one team. You root for one or the other but not both! You've been here for two years; I shouldn't have to tell you that!"

Rich stared out the window. The little Sergeant was going on and on about the city's sports teams. The ride in the backseat was a bumpy one. He could only imagine what it would feel like with a set of hand-cuffs...

"Ok, we are here Rich. Sit tight while I come around and open the door for you. Sorry if this makes you feel like a criminal but hey what can I do? It's company policy. Watch your step. We'll go around to the side entrance.

"Hello Jake..,

"Howdy Malloy. What do you want this time?

"I've got someone here that might be able to I.D. our latest John Doe."

"Well our latest came in ten minutes ago."

"No, not that one."

"You must mean the one shortly after midnight."

"Yeah, where's the body?"

"Follow me gentlemen"

The place was huge and Rich was not enjoying the tour. The place was also freezing. Apparently Sergeant Malloy had done this many times. He seemed at ease as he and his buddy shared a few laughs as they made their way to the back of the tomb like room.

"This is it. Go ahead, take a look," said Jake.

"Is this him Rich?" said Malloy.

"Yes...yes it is. He seems so peaceful now. Sergeant, do you have any idea who did this?"

"I'm afraid not. Sadly most of these types of crimes go unsolved Rich."

"Poor Arnold, he lived all alone in this big city and he was alone when he died," said Rich.

"Does he have any family?"

"He had no one Sergeant. Unless, you consider Seagram's Gin family. Now can we get out of here? This place is making me sick."

"Is this your first time in a morgue?"

"Yes it is and hopefully my last."

"Well you might have to be in one of these at least one more time in your life."

"I'm in no hurry."

"Neither was your friend; I'm afraid. Were you guys close?"

"No, just co-workers, we shared a few laughs but only saw each other at the change of our shift. He was a good man. He didn't deserve to die like this but then again…no one does. Goodbye Arnold."

"Lets head to the precinct; it's only about ten minutes away. I'll get you a ride to the hospital. I'd take you myself but it's not my beat. It wasn't easy seeing your friend like that was it?"

"No it wasn't. I've only seem one dead body my whole life and that was my Great grandmother, she was ninety-five years old. Everyone thought she would live forever. No one else in the family has lived past seventy. How old are you Sergeant?"

"I'm kicking sixty in the rear end. If I make it to seventy, it'll be a miracle."

"That's funny…I would have guessed you were seventy already, simply by the way you walk."

"I got that limp courtesy of a nine year old kid over in Hempstead. I was serving a warrant on his father. I had just put the handcuffs on his old man when I felt a horrific pain in my lower leg. The little fart shot me with his father's 22 pistol! The bullet went straight through my boot and hit my tendon. I couldn't walk for nearly a month and when I did the pain was horrible. If it wasn't for his father the little fart would have shot me again."

"Did you let his father go?"

"I knew you were going to say that. Well... the answer is "absolutely not"! He broke the law and he had to pay his due."

"What did he do?"

"A couple of bad checks at the grocery store a few blocks from his apartment."

"But he just saved your life and that's how you repay him?"

"I felt a little guilty about that at first Rich but then I became angry, that he left his gun where the kid could get it. Trust me, in my line of work a soft heart will get you killed. Here we are. Lets go see the desk Sergeant. He will know who is free to give you a ride.

"Hello Clark...how are you my friend?"

"I'm just fine Malloy."

"I have a gentleman that needs a lift to West Side General. His boss was in a very bad accident and there are no family members to contact. The poor guy fell asleep and hit a utility pole. He's in a coma right now."

"What's your name son?"

"My friends call me Rich."

"Ok Mr. Rich; have a seat on that bench over there and I'll see what I can do."

"Thank you Sergeant."

"Can I talk to you for a minute Malloy?"

"Sure you can Clark."

"Look man, we are not a taxi service. The next time you pull this crap you'll be, completely out of luck."

"Sure thing Clark, that's what you always say. Listen the fellow has had a tough night. He just identified a friend in the morgue and his boss is fighting for his life as we speak. He's one of those Southerners that came up here hoping to strike it rich. I don't think he has another friend in the whole city. Just do this for me and I'll owe you one."

"You mean another one."

"Whatever Clark, look I got to get back on patrol. I'll talk to you later. By the way are we still on for the Yanks and the Mets this weekend?"

"You bet we are you crazy, Met fan."

"I'm not crazy Clark, this is our year...Ok Rich that old Yankee fan over there is going to take care of you. I hope your luck gets better."

"Thank you Sergeant."

"My friends call me Malloy."

"Thanks again for all your help...Malloy."

As Rich watch the little Sergeant proudly limp outside to his huge cruiser he thought to himself. This is who protects the "Big Apple" when everyone is asleep. It wasn't a very comforting thought.

The police station was very busy. Several attractive prostitutes keep the jovial station entertained. Almost thirty minutes later Rich finally heard his name called.

※

"Rich this is Sergeant Milton," said the jolly Yankee fan. He will be giving you a ride to the hospital. I sincerely hope your night gets better."

"Hello Sergeant Milton and thanks for the ride. I really appreciate this."

"No problem mister, word on the street is that you've had a rough night."

"Yeah, I guess I have."

"Which gas station do you operate?"

"It's on 19th and Clover."

"I know that one; it's the one with the old pumps."

"Yes, that's the one."

"It's seems like that gas station has been there forever. I remember it well. They were all set to demolish it about ten years ago. They were going to use the area for parking. If I remember correctly they offered the owner a lot of money to sell but he refused."

"Really...I never heard about that."

"That doesn't surprise me; I'm sure there are a lot of things that you haven't heard about that place. There are some people in that neighborhood that would love to see it torn down. They have complained for years that it's an eye sore but there are others who like what it represents."

"Sergeant what exactly does it represent?"

"The past Rich; you know, "the way things use to be." Some people just can't let go of the past. If I owned the place I wouldn't change a thing except maybe a fresh coat of paint, you know, clean it up a little. I noticed that the garage hasn't had a mechanic in years. How can the place survive just selling gas?"

"Well…I don't think my boss can afford to hire someone to man the garage."

"He wouldn't have to hire a professional mechanic, just an "old school shade tree mechanic" would do. I bet you could even get someone to work that garage for room and board. "Rent is so expensive here." The place does have a room over the top of it doesn't it."

"Yes it does. You seem to know a lot about the old place."

"I'm from the hood." Back in the day that station was thriving. I'm surprised it's not a national landmark. There aren't many stations like that around anymore, especially here in New York. I grew up over on Neck and 23rd, just four blocks away. There was a time though that I was afraid to go any where near that place. I would ride my bike blocks out of the way just so I did come too close to it."

"Why was that?"

"Because of the gas attendant…All of us kids were afraid of that place, so were the adults.

Here's the emergency entrance to the hospital. I'll let you out here. I hope your night gets better Mr. Newell."

"Thanks for the ride Officer and the history lesson but what's this mysterious talk about the gas attendant?"

"Are you telling me that no one has told you the story about the gas attendant?"

"Well now that you mention it. Old Arnold did mention that name a couple of times when he had been drinking. All he would say was the gas attendant is coming back someday real soon. I didn't really know what he meant nor did I care. I just summed it up as a drunken old man talking in riddles. I do however remember Mr. Sanford getting extremely upset with Arnold once and telling him if he mentioned the gas attendant one more time that he was going to fire him. It wasn't the first time that he had threatened to fire Arnold. The old man would just laugh and start humming a strange tune. I do remember Arnold being extremely agitated one morning about three months ago when he couldn't find a wrench that was missing from the tool box. When it appeared two days later, Arnold was happy and said the gas attendant must have been using it. Once again, I just ignored him."

"Well Mr. Newell; I really don't have time to tell you a lot about it but I will say that it's not a myth. The gas attendant is a legend around there. He was a very good mechanic and he was also well liked. He died when the car he was working on fell off the jack. I truly believe his spirit is still hanging around your gas station."

"Why do you believe that?"

"Like I said earlier my friend; I grew up in that neighborhood and most neighborhoods like ours has its fair share of lies that can be linked to the past. However, I assure you that this story is a legitimate one. I have to go now but remember this one thing if you remember nothing else. There are many things in this world that can't be explained but sometimes the easiest things to explain is the hardest thing to believe. Have a good night sir…

"Ok…I'm not sure what that means but I'll think about it. Thanks again for the ride."

"Mr. Newell...

"Yes Sergeant...

"If he comes back...don't be afraid. Spirits can't hurt you, unless you force them."

"Hello Nurse. My name is Richard Newell and I'm here to see Mr. Harold Sanford. I was told that he's in a coma."

"Are you family sir?"

"No but I do work for him."

"I'm sorry but only family members are allowed to see him."

"I understand but the only family that he has is a daughter somewhere in Tennessee and they haven't spoken in years. I've been his employee for the past two years. Doesn't that count for something?"

"It might count for something somewhere sir but the only thing that counts around here is hospital rules. Now please calm down, I'm afraid there is nothing I can do, "its hospital policy."

"Can I please see him for just a few seconds?"

"I'm sorry but the answer is no."

"May I speak to your supervisor?"

"Sure you can but she's only going to repeat what I just said."

"Well can you at least tell me how he's doing?"

"He's in a coma and I'm afraid that's all I can tell you right now."

"Can I use your phone to call a taxi?"

"There's a pay phone at the end of the hall-way."

"Thanks for your help nurse….

"Hello, I need a taxi at West Side General Hospital."

"Where are you going Sir?"

"I'm going to 25 Townsend Street. It's on the East Side."

"Ok, we'll have someone there to get you in about an hour. The fare will be $38.00."

The hour was a long one but the taxi did show.

"Excuse me driver my name is Rich. I know the fare is $38.00 but I only have $34.00 and some change. Can you get me close?"

"Look mister the fare is thirty-eight dollars not a penny less. We are not a charity shuttle."

"I understand that," said Rich. Tomorrow is payday; I can give you the rest then."

"You got to be kidding me right." Get the hell out of my taxi right now!

"Wait, I'm really having a bad night. I lost a friend tonight; he was robbed and killed. I'm at this freaking hospital because my boss had a car accident and is in a coma. They won't let me see him because I'm not family. I could really use a break. I'm living a freaking nightmare right now and I really need to get home. All I'm asking is that you get me close."

"I've got thirty-four bucks. I promise to pay the rest tomorrow; I'll even pay you extra. I work at the gas station on 19th and Clover. Will you please help me?"

"Alright, get back in the car. I'll just have to tell them you were a no show. For thirty-four dollars I can take you to 15 Townsend."

"But that's ten blocks away."

"Take it or leave it fellow!"

"I'll take it."

"Give me the money."

"So your boss is in a coma. I wish my boss were so lucky."

"You don't really mean that."

"Yes I do…you don't know my boss. A coma would be a vast improvement for that, "bitch!"

"Alright mister, if you say so."

"What kind of work you do?

"I run a gas station."

"You're a gas attendant? Ha, ha, that's the only job worst than driving a funky taxi. No harm intended of course. I know times are hard and a man's got to do what a man's got to do. You'll never get rich at that job."

"I'm not trying to get rich friend. I'm just trying to make it."

"Right, right, I can understand that."

"No, I don't think you do. You are charging me thirty-eight dollars to go eleven miles. They have a name for what you are doing, "it's called highway robbery."

"Listen pal, "I don't set the fare." I get a very small percent of it actually, so shut your "piss poor" gas attendant mouth and just ride. If you hate the fare so much buy yourself a car!"

"That's a long story…

As Rich set in the smoke infested yellow taxi, he pondered his future. He briefly considered buying a bus ticket and heading back to Carolina first thing tomorrow. Then he dismissed that idea as quickly as it had arisen. He couldn't go back there, not today, not tomorrow, not ever. For now he would just concentrate on not letting the fat "butter ball" taxi driver choke him to death with his funky cigar…he was exhausted and took a short nap. As Rich slept the driver thought he heard a sob come from the poor guy and he suddenly imagined himself in the gas attendant's shoes. As they crossed the bumpy railroad tracks Rich was jarred awake…

"Hey…wasn't that fifteenth street?"

"Yeah, it was."

"Where are we going?" said Rich.

"Let's just say, your night just got a little better."

Chapter 2

So that taxi driver wasn't such a bad guy after all. He bought me all the way home and told me to forget about the rest of the fare. Too bad he couldn't stick around for a couple of hours and take me to the station.

I had to get some sleep but I could only allow myself to get a few hours. I needed to be on the first bus headed toward the station. My boss might be in a coma but I realized that I had to keep the station running, if for no one else but myself. I packed some extra clothes and some food. I set the alarm for seven and drifted off to sleep for what could not have been more than thirty minutes.

My mind was full of idle thoughts. What was I going to do if Mr. Sanford died? Then a new thought crossed my mind for the first time. There was no one to claim the station but his daughter. I had to try and contact her. I doubted very seriously that she would leave Tennessee to run it; however, there was another option that was the worst of all. Maybe she would sell it. For me that meant certain unemployment. Regardless of my personal problems, I still had to find her. Why had the two of them stopped speaking? What could make a man turn his back on his daughter? Or was it the other way around? Suddenly, I had to know the answer.

When I got to the station, it seemed so empty. Normally Arnold was there but now there was no one but myself. I turned the sign around to read open and waited almost two hours before the first customer came in and all he wanted was a quart of oil and he wanted the cheapest quart that we had.

It was also payday but there was no Mr. Sanford to bring the check. This indeed was a problem. Then it hit me. There was always money at the station. Until now it was simply called emergency funds. Well...I was broke, not a nickel to my name. That classified as an emergency to me.

The money was kept underneath the counter in a well-concealed hole in the floor. I locked the door and took out the small gray box and counted its contents. Five hundred and twenty dollars is what was in that small box. My weekly salary was two hundred dollars. I counted out my share and replaced the rest.

As I replaced the box, I noticed that there was something else in the well-concealed little hole. I took out the object wrapped in an old but expensive handkerchief. It was a small picture of a beautiful young woman lying on a bed with satin sheets. She appeared to be naked underneath the red silk cover. She was beautiful. Why was this picture here? Who is she? I turned the picture over and it simply read, "To the gas attendant with love."

I heard a noise outside. I had a new customer. I quickly returned the picture and the box to their hiding place. I unlocked the door and waited.

This fellow wasn't looking for gas. If I hadn't seen him coming I would have smelled his cheap cologne a mile away. He was dressed in one of those cheap suits that screamed, "I'm the law". When the gentleman finally made his way into the station, it was apparent that his luck had been better somewhere in the not to distant past.

He was well groomed and had an air about him that made you believe he was somebody. If not for the cheap cologne and tattered suit, he could have easily pulled it off.

I was ready for whatever he threw my way. He made it simple.

"Good morning my name is Detective Gray."

"Hello Detective, what can I do for you?"

"I'd like to speak to the owner."

"I'm afraid that's not possible at the moment. Is there anything that I can assist you with?"

"What's your name?"

"It's Richard Newell but my friends call me Rich."

"Ok Richie, I'm following up on the Arnold case."

"I'd really prefer it, if you didn't call me Richie."

"Of course, I apologize, now let me see… according to my notes an employee of this fine establishment identified the recently deceased at the morgue last night."

"That was me."

"How well did you know the deceased?"

"Not well at all but better than most."

"Who were his friends?"

"Don't know that he had any. We were co-workers, I didn't know much about his private life. He worked twelve-hour shifts here seven days a week. This place was his life at least for the past twenty years. Before that I don't know what he did."

"Well, I know what he did. Your friend had just spent fifteen years at Riker's Island before becoming employed at this fine establishment."

"Arnold was no felon!"

"Sure he was. The old guy pleaded guilty to two counts of murder. He even turned himself in. It was an open and shut case. The judge actually felt sorry for the poor guy and cut him a great plea deal."

"I'm having trouble believing any of this."

"I know it's hard for you to believe but it's true. He killed his best friend and his wife. I don't have to tell you why...do I." The story went like this. Arnold had been working at Hillside hospital for over eleven years. He was always on time and had recently been promoted to supervise the second shift maintenance crew. During this time he had become friends with a drifter who went by the initials of D.C.

Arnold had interviewed D.C. and recommend that he be hired. After getting him the job Arnold also let him move in with him and his wife for a few months, until D.C. saved enough money to find his own place.

D.C. worked very hard for Arnold and quickly gained his trust. They started hanging out at after hour's bars when they got off work. At this time your friend Arnold wasn't a big drinker and it was easy to get him drunk. D.C. would always make sure that Arnold made it home safely.

Arnold's wife was a seamstress from Brooklyn. She had a nice set of twins on her but was lacking in the booty department but was the sweetest woman you could ever hope to meet. She was also a terrific cook. She and Arnold had been married for six years and she had been faithful to him the entire time.

On this particular night, she was mad at D.C. because he was keeping her husband out too late. She demanded that he leave. As she fussed at him, D.C. actually started to become aroused as her bosom heaved up and down as she yelled at him. He noticed that the more she yelled the longer and harder her nipples seemed to get. Suddenly he wanted to screw her brains out. He made an advance at her a few nights later when Arnold was passed out sloppy drunk on the couch. She tried to fight him off but he was too strong. D.C. held her down on the kitchen table with a knife to her neck. He raised her dress, removed her panties with his teeth and started to pleasure her with his tongue.

Moans of joy escaped her lips as he caressed her clitoris with his lips and tongue. Arnold had never pleased her in this way. She grabbed D.C's head and held it close to her vagina. She screamed out in pleasure as he softly sucked the juices from her love zone. The woman from Brooklyn that had attended church and bible study faithfully for the past twenty-four years was in love for the first time in her life. Until now, Arnold had been her only lover but she suddenly realized that he wasn't making LOVE to her at all...

After this D.C. started missing a lot of time at work. He pleasured her as she liked and showed her how to pleasure him also. Apparently, his penis wasn't any bigger than Arnold's but the way he used it delighted her completely... she now understood what all the talk about "the motion in the ocean" was all about! She had fallen in love with D.C. and made sure he was completely satisfied thus neglecting Arnold's advances completely.

Six months later she told Arnold that she wanted a divorce. She also told him that she was in love with another man. Arnold took the news hard. The only person that he felt comfortable confiding in was his friend D.C...

I don't have to tell you what his friend advised him to do...

"I'm speechless," said Rich.

"I know...hard to believe isn't it? I guess you never really know anyone. Explains why he spent so many years working here for pennies a day doesn't it. Most ex-cons can never get a decent paying job when they get out, especially the ones that commit murder."

"I'm shocked."

"Don't be my boy. This is New York. The city is full of felons. Most appear to be nice people, some even manage to put the past behind them and go on to live respectful lives. The percentage is small though. The city is hard enough for the normal guy, you throw in a felony conviction and it becomes Satan's paradise on earth."

"Wow and I thought I had it bad."

"I only have one more question for you Richie, I mean Rich and then, I'll be on my way."

"What is it detective?"

"Where were you last night around midnight?"

"I was right here detective." I was right here; mad as a Carolina Catfish that just realized the juicy red worm it had swallowed had a rusty hook attached to it; all this unnecessary anguish I directed toward Arnold for being late, it never (sob) crossed my mind that he was laying on a street corner six blocks away dead!"

"Can anyone verify that?"

"Come on, give me a break, I can't believe you suspect me."

"I'm only doing my job son. I have to cover every possibility. Now tell me how things were between Arnold and yourself."

"Things were just fine between us!"

"No need to raise your voice friend. I'll be in touch if I have any more questions."

"Do me a favor detective."

"What is that Rich?"

"Find his killer!"

"Sorry son, I'd be a fool to make that promise but I will try.' Have a good day Rich."

"You find his killer detective!

I looked around me and saw this place for the first time. It was filthy. I thought about what the officer had said about this place thriving in its hay day. It was hard for me to imagine but no harder than imagining Arnold as a murderer. Your wife and your best friend sleeping together in your bed, now that's a hard pill to swallow. How does that happen? Poor Arnold, I wonder how long it was going on before he found out?

I picked up a broom and started the tedious task of sweeping up the place. After about twenty minutes, I looked out the window and noticed that Marvin had hooked up to the under ground gas tanks and was heading my way.

Marvin was the route driver for our gas supplier. He desperately needed to do some crunches and it would also help my piece of mind if he stopped smoking his freaking cigarette when he was filling the tanks. He was of Irish decent but you couldn't tell by looking at him.

He had been on the route for the past ten years and he wasn't the nicest person that you'd ever meet. He was a company man, which meant strictly business. He accounted for every single ounce of gas that he put in our tanks. The bill reflected that.

"Good Morning Marvin."

"Hi Rich, what are you doing in?"

"I'm afraid that Arnold went and got himself killed yesterday."

"Oh no man; you're pulling my leg right?"

"I'm afraid not."

"Dang, I hate to hear that. I liked Arnold. I liked him very, very much. How's old man Sanford taking the news?"

"That's another thing Marvin; Mr. Sanford ran his car into a utility pole on the very same night that Arnold was murdered. He was actually on his way in to work for Arnold because we hadn't heard from him."

"Well dang… now this is a lot to swallow this early in the morning Rich. How's the old fellow doing?"

"He's in a coma."

"What you say? A coma…my God, I better shut off the pumps."

"Wait Marvin, where you going so fast?"

"I can't fill these tanks today Rich. Your boss is in a coma. Who's going to pay for this gas? I'm sorry but I'll have to clear it with the main office before I put one more drop in your tanks."

"Come on Marvin, we only have enough gas to last about three days. What are we going to do?"

"Sorry Richie, it's out of my hands. Oh by the way which hospital is the old man in."

"He's at West Side General."

"Why that's clear across town."

"Yeah Marvin, I know."

After he left I measured the amount of gas in the tanks. It's a good thing that he couldn't remove the gas that he had just put in. I did the calculations and it look as though we had enough gas to last six maybe seven days. What would I do when we ran out?

I called the hospital but all they would tell me is that he was still my in a coma. That was all I really needed to know I guess because it meant he was still alive.

I had decided that I needed to do two things. First, I should try to get into Mr. Sanford's home. There had to be a way to reach his daughter and the answer was somewhere inside his house. The second thing was to find someone to help run this garage. I placed an ad in the Long Island Press for a mechanic/gas attendant. Pay would be room and board plus three meals a day. "If only I had it so good"

Two days later Marvin returned with apologies galore. He said when he told his boss about Mr. Sanford, they threatened to fire him on the spot if he didn't return ASAP and fill our tanks. His boss said that Mr. Sanford had never been late paying his bill and instructed Marvin to keep the tanks full. It was a good thing because in three days our tanks would have been bone dry.

After a couple of hours of intense brain storming, I convinced myself that I had to get into Mr. Sanford house. I had a ring full of keys; maybe one of them fit his house. If they didn't work I'd just have to go through a window. Either way it had to be done. He didn't live in a ritzy neighborhood so there wasn't much chance of him having an alarm but then again, maybe that was more the reason to have one.

In my mind I thought about all the things that could go wrong but I knew I have to continue. I owed it to my boss to contact his daughter.

I wonder if his neighbors knew what happened to him. How could they? They weren't family but were they close? Had anyone been keeping an eye on his place? As I approached the back door I had my answer. No one was keeping an eye on this place but someone had definitely been here since the accident and they had not bothered to close the back door, unless they were still here.

This didn't feel right. Maybe, I should just come back tomorrow during the daylight hours. No, I couldn't pay another taxi to bring me back tomorrow; that would be a stupid waste of money. There was no turning back now.

As I stepped inside the door I felt a sudden cold rush, slowly sneak past me. My heart skipped a beat and I suddenly found myself too terrified to take another step. The door slammed shut behind me and I lunged for the wall quickly groping the wall in search of a light switch. To my sudden delight I found the switch.

As the bright lights filled the empty darkness I found that my hands were trembling beyond belief. My forehead was suddenly dripping with sweat and my heart was beating so loud and so fast that I thought it was going to burst through my chest! Dear God! What was that?

Something or someone had been in this room with me.

Why I stayed in that house at that moment is beyond me. I knew I had to finish what I can here for. As I moved from room to room I turned on the lights.

Probably a stupid move on my part but if there was something or someone in this house, I wanted them to know that I was here also. If a neighbor noticed the lights and called the police I would deal with that problem at that time.

The house was old but neat. Everything seemed to have its own place. It was nothing like the station. I decided that the answer about the daughter had to be in his bedroom upstairs. I slowly ascended the staircase and every time I stepped on the old wood, it cried out in pain but the stairs were spotless.

There were two bedrooms and it was clear which one was being used. I suddenly remembered that the old people in my family use to hide their valued papers either in the closet or under the bed in a small chest. If he had any record of his daughter it should be in one of those places.

Mr. Sanford had made it easy for me. I found what I was looking for immediately. There was a small chest on the top shelf in the back corner of the closet. The closet was large enough to sleep in but it was also full of spider webs; quite a contrast to the rest of the house. I took the chest and placed it on the bed.

Was this going too far? Whatever was in this chest was private and opening it would be worst than breaking into this house. I convinced myself that I had no choice. I couldn't turn back now, besides, if I didn't try to find his daughter who would?

I slowly opened the box and carefully began my journey through his personal belonging. There were lots of receipts folded neatly, several deeds for land but mostly old pink and yellow faded papers with unreadable print. Then I saw what I was looking for. It must have been how the old gold diggers felt when they saw the first sign of a gold nugget.

It was a picture with two smiling faces on it. There was a little girl about ten years old and a very pretty woman who I guessed was Mr. Sanford's late wife who he often spoke of. Strangely, the corner of the picture was torn off. I could make out the form of a man but the face had purposely been torn off.

Was the missing face in the picture Mr. Sanford? It had to be, there weren't many people shaped like he was. If you took a bowling ball and attached some arms, legs and a smiling face, you would have Mr. Sanford.

Why had someone left the faceless body with its arm around the beautiful woman's shoulders? Furthermore how was a man like him able to get a woman like his wife? She was beautiful. Her body was very curvaceous and her face was perfect. Something just didn't add up here...

I flipped the picture over; it was dated the spring of 69. There were three names Willie, Lilly and Elizabeth. Next to the picture was a certified letter that had been addressed to Elizabeth four years ago. It had been returned unopened. It had a Tennessee address and phone number written on the back.

I picked up the phone and then put it back down. A million thoughts were going through my head. I now had an address, a phone number and a name. What would I say to her if she answered the phone?

I decided that there was no easy way to say your father's in a coma. So I dialed the number and waited for someone to pick up. On the fourth ring I got an answer.

"Hello"

"Hello, I'm looking for Elizabeth."

"This is she. How may I help you?"

"My name is Richard Newell. I work for your father. I'm afraid that he's been in a bad accident."

"Is this some kind of sick joke mister? My father died fifteen years ago."

"Am I speaking to Elizabeth Sanford?"

"Sanford was my maiden name."

"I'm Elizabeth Elkhart now."

"Do you know a Mr. Harry Sanford?"

"Yes, he was my father. Who are you and what is this about?"

"Well...I'm trying to reach his daughter. She is the only family that I know of. It's really important. Right now he's in the hospital and he's in a coma. I'm not sure how much longer he will live. Are you sure you're not his daughter?"

"I told you my father died fifteen years ago. I'm sorry, I can't help you. Now it's late...please don't call here again, you have the wrong number."

"Ok but can you answer one question for me?"

"What is it?"

"How did your father die?"

"He was shot in the face with a shotgun. Now please it's late, don't call here again."

"Liz who was that?" said Henry.

"I don't know. Let's go back to sleep."

Elizabeth couldn't go back to sleep. She wanted to know how someone was finally able to find her after forty years. Who was that man she thought and what is happening in New York?

I put the picture in my pocket and headed downstairs. I decided to have a quick look around and make sure everything was locked up. I was more confused now than ever. I found a spare set of keys that I was sure were to the house. I put them in my pocket.

It was obvious that I would have to take care of things around here. I turned out all the lights and just before I left I decided to check the garage and made a startling discover.

I opened the door and couldn't believe my eyes. Sitting in the middle of the garage was a midnight blue 1956 Chevy. The car was in mint condition.

Like a kid with his first go-cart on Christmas day, I climbed behind the wheel and imagined myself cruising through Manhattan. Mr. Sanford had never mentioned he had a car like this. He always drove the old Ford Fairlane to work. Does this car run? It didn't look like it had been out of this garage in over thirty years but the inside was clean.

Where is the key to this beautiful car? I tried every key on the spare key ring but none of them fit. Then I decided to look in the ashtray and there it was. I picked it up and with trembling fingers I slowly put it into the ignition and turned the key.

Without hesitation the beautiful beast roared to life. What a sweet sound! Mozart would be so jealous.

I pulled on the lights and the garage lit up like Time's Square on New Year's Eve. The gas needle was sitting on full. My next thought was the craziest one yet but I acted on it the quickest. I jumped out of the car, raised the garage door and pulled the Chevy into the street. I closed the door and headed for the station. Except for a slight pull to the right when I pressed the brake peddle, the big car drove magnificently. It was definitely not my little 1982 Porsche, "oh how I missed that little car." It was great to be driving again.

Should I go to jail for my actions the past three hours?" thought Rich. Maybe, but one thing was certain. I could take care of his gas station better with his car. As far as I was concerned they were a package deal. I'll deal with any consequences at a later time. Besides, the only person that might complain would be Mr. Sanford and it didn't look like that would be happening any time soon.

I parked the car at the station. I felt as though I had stepped back in time. This gas station and that car were from the same place in time. Wow, Mr. Sanford what a beautiful secret. What else are you hiding?

It was 6:00am. I went inside and turned the sign around to read open. I stared out the window at the 56 Chevy and wondered how my boss was doing.

I took the picture out of my pocket and taped it to the counter. I looked at the two smiling faces again. I'm sure the missing face was Mr. Sanford but his name was Harry not Willie. Who was Willie?

There were so many questions and no answers. I was tired and I wanted to sleep. I didn't want to see any customers; I just wanted a comfortable bed but that wasn't going to happen any time soon. Business at the place was good today. It would have been great except I had to turn away a few customers because I didn't have a mechanic. It had been four days since I placed the ad but I hadn't received one call about it.

Everyone commented on the Chevy. It really was a piece of art. I think if I every paint again, my first painting will include a picture of it.

My customers felt like I did. The car belonged at the station they said. Some even commented that they only stopped because of it but it was my afternoon customer that was the most intrigued by it. Her name was Teresa and her fascination with the Chevy was a thing to behold.

She was a pretty woman, probably in her mid twenties. She dressed like a Tom Boy but it was very obvious that she was all woman especially, when she bent over to pick up a dime off the ground.

Most people were content to just admire the Chevy from the outside but she wanted to look under the hood. So I obliged her. It didn't take a rocket scientist to realize that this wasn't her first tour of this mighty engine. By the time she was finished, it was clear that love at first sight does exist. If that car were a man, it would be lying on its back right now, with a huge smile on its face.

She bought a quart of oil and five dollars worth of gas. When she left her blue rustic Honda was blowing blue smoke from the exhaust and the brakes were crying out for help. The rotors were shot; even my non-mechanical brain knew that. It was surprising to see the car stop at all. That poor girl needed a mechanic in the worst way.

My first week at the station had netted a lousy $780.56. I subtracted my weekly salary of $200.00 and put the rest in the emergency funds box and tucked it safe away. By the time I paid my rent I would only have $40.00 left. Then I suddenly had an idea. I closed up shop and drove to my one room apartment.

I went inside the apartment building and took the elevator to the third floor and then took the stairs down one flight. The elevator never stopped on the second floor and I couldn't get to my room from the staircase on the first floor.

As I approached my room I noticed a letter taped to the door. It was from Miss Wilson. She was demanding the rent, which totaled $325.00. That price included the following week's rent but I wouldn't be here come next week.

I gathered my belonging and stuffed them into my laundry bags. I left what I owed her and a notice that I was vacating the apartment, effective immediately. I suddenly realized how little I had in this world. I threw the two laundry bags in the trunk of the Chevy and headed to the hospital.

I had the picture with me. I wasn't sure how much good it would do a man in a coma but maybe when he comes out of it the picture might be of some comfort.

Once again I was told family only. At least this time I really felt that the nurse wanted to let me see him but she wasn't about to risk her job to do so. I gave her the picture and I thought I saw a tear fill her left eye. She said that she would make sure he got it. I believed her.

Chapter 3

My sleeping arrangements had to change. The sofa was killing my back. It was time to start cleaning the room over the garage. None of the keys fit the lock so I used a pair of rustic bolt cutters that had seen better days. Finally after wrestling with the lock for several minutes, I was able to get into the room.

I had never been in this room. As far as I can remember it had always been locked. I often wondered why but was never stupid enough the ask old man Sanford. I stepped inside and looked at my new living quarters. It would do just fine, and you couldn't beat the rent.

There was an old zenith TV in the corner. The room had a large window that faced the front of the station. Because the room was on the second floor there was also a view of Peterman's park. The park was nothing special. It had been abandoned by the city years ago. However, some of the locals had taken it upon themselves to keep it up. The room was probably fourteen feet by sixteen feet. A room this size normally went for about two hundred a week here. Throw in a view of the park and you could add another fifty bucks.

The bed was small but in excellent condition. I decided to get rid of the sheets and pillows. Although the sheets appeared to be very expensive they were old but still better than anything that I had ever slept on. They appeared to be silk. What an odd place for silk sheets, I thought.

The walls needed a fresh coat of paint. I went into the bathroom and flushed the toilet. It worked perfectly, however the dark color of the water was a little alarming.

I turn on the faucet to the face bowl and it ran brown water for over a minute and then suddenly the water became as clear as a bottle of Dasani's finest.

The doorbell rang and I rushed downstairs. To my surprise there stood Sergeant Malloy with a small grin on his face.

"Hello Richie, how are you doing on this fine afternoon?"

"Given the circumstances; I'm just fine Sergeant. What can I do for you?"

"Well...I was wondering, if you've heard from his family yet?"

"No...I'm afraid that I haven't."

"That's too bad. The poor guy has been in that damn coma for a week now. You would think that someone would have called by now."

"Not really Sergeant; he only has the one daughter. As far as I know they haven't spoken in years. I thought I told you that already."

"Yes, you did mention that. Hey...is that your 57 Chevy?"

"It's a 56 Chevy and it belongs to Mr. San-ford."

"I see...so you're driving it?"

"Yeah, I have to take care of his home and check in on him at the hospital. The car makes things easier."

"It's a nice machine. I've always been a Ford man myself but the 57 Chevy is a classic."

"Yes it is Sergeant, so is the 56."

"Look if you hear from that daughter; tell her to give me a call. Here's my card."

"If I hear from her Sergeant, you'll be the first to know."

"Ok then Rich, have a good day."

"Thanks Sergeant, I'll try."

As the little policeman slowly walked back to his car, Rich noticed that he had left a trail of sunflower seeds behind him.

I grabbed a broom and a dustpan and went back upstairs. The place was dirtier than it looked. It took me almost two hours of sweeping, dusting and mopping to get the floor clean but when I was finished I was very pleased.

I rigged up a bell in the room so that I could hear the customers when they drove into the station. This turned out to be a great way to get some sleep and run the station. The next day I painted the walls of my new living quarters. It turned out to be the hardest project of all. The walls just sucked up the paint.

I had to go get more paint. I made a list of what I needed and headed to Wally-World or as some people might say Wal-Mart. When I returned an hour later there was a note on the door inquiring about the mechanic position. There was no contact number; the person wrote that they would return later. I went upstairs and continued to paint the walls. I was almost finished when I heard laughter coming from outside. I looked out the window and saw three boys that appeared to be drunk standing beside the Chevy. Then I saw one of them take a brick and throw it at the car. I rushed outside and the young punks ran down the street.

I slowly approached the car and noticed that the passenger side window was broken. I looked the car over closely and that appeared to be the only damage. I had to get the car inside the garage. Why hadn't I thought of this earlier?

As long as I had worked here, I have never seen the garage doors open. When I went inside and tried to open it, I saw why. The wood where the hinges were attached on one side was completely rotted. I knew there was no way that I could fix that tonight or any other night.

The entire door would have to be replaced. I also noticed that there were two large rusty chains attached to each side of the garage. It was apparent that Mr. Sanford hadn't wanted the garage door to be opened for a very long time. I would need more than the rustic bolt cutters for this job.

I moved the car closer to the door; crawled behind the huge wheel and locked all the doors. It was 1:00a.m.; this would be my bed for the night. I guess you can say I got kind of lucky because I was able to sleep uninterrupted for the next six hours.

Later that morning, I called around to get an estimate for the garage door. I finally settled on Mario's Garage Installers. They specialized in the older garages. Mr. Mario said they could do the job for $400.00 dollars. He assured me that it was a deal. I checked the emergency funds. By the end of the day, the old place had a new garage door. I pulled the Chevy inside and locked the door.

I thought cleaning the room upstairs was a chore. This service garage was the worst. Why did Mr. Sanford let it get this bad? I tossed the dust pan aside. For this job I would need a shovel. I headed to the utility shed in the back. As I stepped outside I was startled when someone called out to me.

I looked in the direction that the voice was coming from and immediately recognized my visitor. It was the girl with the smoking Honda. I looked around but the Honda was nowhere in sight.

"Do you remember me from last week?" she said.

"Yeah, I remember you. What can I do for you today?"

"I'm here about the job."

"What job?"

"Sir, I'm referring to the mechanic's position that you have posted on your door."

"You're a mechanic?"

"I don't have any fancy papers that say I am but I know my way around an engine better than most men do. I can change oil, repair brakes and pretty much anything else."

"What's your name again?"

"It's Teresa but my friends call me Resa."

"Well Resa; judging from the mechanical state of that Honda you were driving, I'd say your mechanical ability rates somewhere next to mine and I'm afraid that's not going to be good enough."

"First of all Mr. Newell, anyone will tell you that mechanics have the worst maintenance records when it come to their own cars. Secondly, that Honda was a piece of horse manure. It was a great car in its day but that was three hundred thousand miles ago."

"That car had that many miles on it? Amazing my Porsche only had fifty-thousand when it let me down."

"Yes it did. It was a hand me down from my father. Only good thing he did for me my whole life."

"Where is it now?"

"Out on Southern State Parkway, where I left it after the engine blew this morning."

"How did you get here?"

"I took the train to downtown and walked the rest of the way."

"That's quite a hike Resa; you must be exhausted. Would you like a soda pop?"

"The hike was nothing Rich and the soda would be greatly appreciated, "if it's free". Now about this job…your ad says room and board". What is your idea of room and board?"

"That would be three meals a day, a pillow and a place to wash your face Resa. Not really the best life style for a woman now is it?"

"If you add $50.00 dollars a week you got yourself a mechanic…I can start today."

"Wait a minute, slow down. I need references, plus I have to do a background check. Come inside so I can write down your information."

"Alright, where's the Chevy?"

"It's in the garage. I had some trouble last night. Some kids were trying to use it for target practice."

"Can I see it?"

"Sure…right this way."

"Hey, I see you got yourself a new garage door."

"I had no choice. Couldn't afford it either."

"I understand, these old stations don't make a lot of money but if they are managed right they can do pretty good. It looks like they smashed the passenger side window pretty bad. That'll cost you about five or six hundred dollars unless you get lucky and find one at the junkyard."

"What? Five hundred dollars you say. I can't afford that. Tell me about this junkyard."

"Well…there's a great junkyard out by Shea Stadium. That's where I get all my parts. I know this guy out there named Charles and he's kind of sweet on me, "if you know what I mean." He always gives me a break on the prices. I could probably get you that window for less than fifty bucks.

"Really…less than fifty bucks, now that would be great."

I can also get you a master cylinder for the brakes for about that same price."

"What makes you think the car needs brake work?"

"I bet when you apply the brakes the car pulls to the right slightly...doesn't it?"

"Yes it does. How do you know that?"

"It was a flaw with the 56 Chevy. They didn't fix it until the 58 model came out. The owners didn't complain at first because it wasn't a big deal, "unless you had to suddenly slam on the brakes." I can fix the window and the brakes for you. All you have to do is hire me."

"You're quite a negotiator."

"I'm an even better mechanic."

"You say that window can cost me six hundred bucks?"

"The car is a classic. Of course they are going to charge you an arm and a leg for that window."

You're sure you can get me that window for that price Resa."

"If they have it, I can. Why don't we ride out there later today and see."

"I have too much work to do. I'm trying to clean out the garage right now."

"It's pretty bad in here Rich, it'll take you all day, unless you hire some help and I don't see anyone beating down your door for that job."

"Well that's one thing you're right about. Why should they be, the pay stinks."

"Yes it does...ha, ha."

"Where are you from Resa?"

"I'm proud to say that I'm from South Jersey."

"How old are you?"

I'm twenty-four in three weeks."

"You're not an escaped convict or a felon are you?"

"Well...Rich, I'm not an escaped convict but as far as the felon part, it depends on who you ask."

"Well...I'm asking you."

"When I was twenty, "I stole a tank of gas and a couple of snickers when I was driving through Ohio. I waited inside while the old geezer filled the tank. When he came inside, I ran and jumped in the car. I didn't know the old fart could move so fast. He took his shotgun and shot out the back of my window as I sped away. I'll never do that again and I haven't been back to Ohio since."

"That's probably a good idea. I don't really think that's the kind of information that you'd want to put on any employment applications in the future."

Ding, ding…

"Sounds like you have a customer at the pumps. Can I help him?"

"Okay, but I'm watching you."

"Good morning Sir. How can I help you to-day?"

"I need ten dollars worth of regular and an orange soda."

"Okay, that's not a problem. Would you like me to check your oil?"

"Check my oil?' Why I haven't heard anyone say that in years."

"Well we decided it was time to bring back good old-fashioned service. It looks like you have plenty of oil but you should think about changing it soon. Come back next week and we'll change it for you."

"Are you saying that you're opening up the old garage?"

"Yes we are."

"That's hard to believe young lady. Are you really going to open the garage?"

"That's what I said Sir."

"Are you trying to make someone roll over in their grave?"

"Why...do you say that?"

"You're new around aren't you?"

"Yes, this is my first day."

"Young lady my name is Kenneth Collins and I live about six blocks from here. I was here when they had ground breaking. That was a great day for this neighborhood...but that was before things went so wrong. I don't even know why I still come to this old haunted place."

"Haunted...what are you saying?"

"Young lady don't you know what happen here?"

"No I don't."

"Well…if I were you. I'd have a talk with the owner about that garage or better yet, I'd be looking for a new job that's far away from that garage. As far as I'm concerned opening that garage is like opening a doorway to the past but it's a door that should remain closed! How much I owe you?"

"Ten dollars for the gas and fifty cent for the soda…

"Here's eleven bucks young lady; you can keep the change."

"Thank you and I hope to see you next week so we can change that oil."

"Don't hold your breath on that one. I'll never allow my car to be pulled into that garage. If I were you young lady, I'd get far away from here and find myself another job."

"Look Rich a ten dollar bill."

"That's a pretty good sale on your first try young lady. Come on, I'll show you how to operate the register."

"I already know how. I'll show you. He bought one orange soda, which is fifty-cent and nine dollars worth of gas. He also gave me a fifty-cent tip. By the way, that gentleman might be back next week for an oil change."

"Really... that's great news, I guess you're hired. I better show you to your room. Let's go upstairs. I've been working up here a little for the past two days."

"Do I smell fresh paint?"

"That's right, I just finished last night. I was planning for this to be my room."

"Rich this is a nice room but it's missing two very important things."

"What's missing?"

"It needs a small fridge and a lock on that door."

"I'll get you a fridge tomorrow and I'll fix the lock later today." "When do you want to move in?"

"Tonight, I'll get my stuff in a day or two."

"Okay...I guess that means I'm back to sleeping on the sofa...Let's have a soda before we tackle the garage. What kind you want?"

"A coke will be fine.

"Here you go Resa. I'm going to back the Chevy out so we can get started."

"Can I do it?"

"You're not going to run off in it are you?"

"No, I'm not. I'm starting to wish I had never told you that story."

"I'm glad you did. That's my boss car, you run off with it and we'll both be in trouble."

"Where is he?"

"He's in the hospital."

"What's wrong with him?"

"He hit a utility pole on his way into work last week."

"Is he going to be ok?"

"I don't know, he's in a coma and they won't let me see him because I'm not family. The only family he has is a daughter somewhere in Tennessee but no one knows where."

"That's so sad."

"Here are the keys Resa. Remember it's not a Honda."

"Rich…

"Yes Resa."

"Why has this garage been locked and unused for so long?"

"I don't know Resa, when I started here two years ago it wasn't being used. I know Mr. Sanford was looking for a mechanic when he hired me but after he hired me he took down the sign and nothing was ever said about it."

"So you've been here two years."

Yes, "that's right."

"Do you like it here?"

"No, the pay is terrible and so are the hours."

"So why don't you leave."

"I don't know Resa, it's hard to explain. Sometimes, I feel like the place doesn't want me to leave."

"Rich is this place haunted?"

"Ha, ha, what a silly question...Why would you even say such a thing?"

"Well…never mind. I think it will be a good idea if we went to the junkyard and looked for that window."

"You might be right about that. We can finish this when we get back."

"Do you have any tools Rich?"

"Sure the one thing that this place has is plenty of tools."

"Great…throw them in the trunk and lets go before it gets too late."

"Rich, this is the exit coming up, you better slow down or you'll miss it."

"Yes, I can feel how the car was pulling to the right just now."

"How many miles are on this car?"

"It has almost thirty thousand."

"Wow, it's practically brand new."

"Not really Resa, these cars were not built to take the kind of punishment that the cars today do. It was very rare to see one of these with a huge amount of miles."

"That's true in a sense Rich but people just didn't know how to take care of their cars back then."

"How much further Resa?"

"Go to Northern blvd, which is less than half a mile and take a right. It will take us right past Shea Stadium. Have you been to a game since you've been here?"

"No I haven't, I'm not much of a fan."

"That's too bad, there's not a better way to past the time than at a baseball game."

"I thought the point of going to the game was to watch the game."

"It is sort of but there are so many things going on at the game. Maybe we can go together someday and I can show you."

"Okay Resa, we'll do that."

"Follow this street and take the second right. There are a lot of small junkyards within this huge junkyard. When we get there we'll want to go to the one near the back. Slow down, here's the entrance."

"Wow, this is quite a place. It's nothing like I imagined. Look at all the rims," said Rich.

"Yeah watch out for these guys, they are pretty aggressive salesmen. If you're not careful this Chevy will have dubs on it before you know it," laughed Resa.

"Lady, I seriously doubt that, dubs cost a lot of money, even in the junkyard."

"Yeah Rich that's true but these people out here are after money and they will make you a deal. This Chevy would look nice with the right set."

"Just point the way to the window Resa, there will be no dubs."

"Pull over to that one on your left. We should be able to get a good deal here. The owner is kind of sweet on me. Just let me do the talking."

"Hi, Charles, how are you?"

"Hello Resa, it's always a pleasure to have your beautiful face...grace my place. Is that Honda giving you problems again?"

Rich watched in awe as Resa and Charles greeted each other. This man was a dead ringer for the leading character in that book called "Sleepy Hollow". Charles had big ears, a goofy smile and when he opened his mouth to laugh at something that Resa had said, Rich counted three large teeth across the top and three large teeth on the bottom. Each set had a large gap between each tooth. Charles had to be at least six foot, six inches tall. He was as skinny as a rail. The only thing missing was a horse to complete the scene.

"No, I'm afraid that its days of giving me trouble are over but it did finally stop running."

"That sounds like a problem to me," laughed Charles.

"On most days it would be Charles but not today. I want you to meet my boss."

"Did you say your boss? Boss of what?" smiled Charles as the wiped his hands on his trousers.

"You heard right, I got me a job over in Hempstead, working at a garage. Rich this is Mr. Charles Edwards and he owns this here junkyard."

"Hello, it's nice to meet you Charles."

"Hey mister any friend of Resa, is a friend of mine. What can I do for you today?"

"See that Chevy."

"Yeah, I noticed that 57 as soon as you pulled up. It's a beautiful car. They don't make them like that anymore. My Grandfather had one."

"Well…I think it's a 56," said Rich. You are right. They don't make them like that anymore."

"No Rich, that's a 57," said Charles.

"Do you have any in the yard?" said Resa.

"Yeah Resa, I think there might be a couple of those cars in the rear corner but they are pretty stripped. What are you looking for?"

"We need a passenger side window and a brake cylinder."

"Good luck finding either of those but if I have it, I'll take $125.00 for the window and $75.00 for the cylinder."

"We'll give you $90.00 for both," smiled Resa.

"Come on lady, I don't have time to play this game with you today. Why don't you just steal those parts from me? I'd feel better."

"Well…just forget about the cylinder, I'll just jimmy rig it."

"What's wrong with the brakes?"

"The owner never replaced the original Master cylinder."

"Oh is that all, It pulls to the right a little doesn't it. I know lots of people that never changed that. It'll be fine. Leave it alone Resa. I know you."

"Okay, maybe you're right; we'll give you fifty bucks for that window, if you have it."

"It's a good thing that you don't come here everyday. I'd go bankrupt. Excuse me; it looks like I got some more customers. I hope they aren't thieves too."

"Go get the tool box out of the car Rich. Let's hope that they have one."

"How often do you come here?"

"Well when I had the Honda I came here a couple of times a month. It had a lot of miles on it. It always needed something. Old Charles is kind of sweet on me. He once sold me an entire engine for only twenty bucks. He's a nice enough person but not my type at all. Besides, the engine was just lying over there on the ground. The rings were completely gone in it but I drove it for six months."

"Twenty bucks that sounds like a deal. How much was it to get someone to put the engine in for you?"

"Nothing, I did it myself Rich."

"Really...

"Yes, I thought I told you; I'm a mechanic."

"Hey look Resa, here's one."

"No Rich that's a 58 but help me raise the hood. No parts on this one. No doors either."

"Your friend Charles was right; it looks like everything back here is stripped. There's another one over there."

"Let's go take a closer look at it. Now this one is a 56 isn't it?"

"It's hard to tell Rich. They look so much alike but let's raise the hood."

"Wouldn't you know it," said Resa. It still has a master cylinder."

"This one is a bust also little lady but it does have its doors."

"Yeah but the windows are either missing or cracked."

"It looks like we are out of luck, I don't see any others."

"Me either but that doesn't mean there isn't another one out here. Rich most yards like to put the same type of cars in the same place but sometimes the workers might just leave the car in another location for whatever reason, so you just have to walk around and hope that you get lucky. Let's go look over there."

"I hope you don't mind my asking but it's not normal to see a female mechanic. How did you get involved with cars?"

"My grandfather was a mechanic. He use to take me everywhere with him. Poor fellow couldn't afford a decent car, so most of our time together was spent in his garage working on his car. Once he had fixed whatever the problem was, we would always go on a test drive to the local grocery store. Sometimes we made it, sometimes we didn't. This went on for years."

One day we were out driving and just before we got home the radiator hose burst. It looked worst than it was. I thought the car was on fire but my grandfather just keep on driving as though everything was fine.

When we got home, he parked it under the maple tree and raised the hood. Then he picked me up, put me own his shoulders and carried me into the house. I said granddad isn't we going to fix the car? He said later child, I'm tired right now.

The car set out there under the tree all night. The next morning my Uncle Thomas came over and took my grandfather to the hospital where he stayed for three days. While he was in the hospital I decided that I would fix the car for him.

"How old were you?"

"I was eight."

"Did you fix it?"

"Well...no but I made a valiant attempt. I found a new hose in the trunk. I guess my grandfather knew that hose was going to burst soon. It took me all day to get that hose off the car but it only took me a few minutes to put the new one on."

"I'm sorry Resa but I believe that you are pulling my leg with this story."

"I know that's what everyone that I've told this story to thinks. The only person that believed me was my grand father."

When he came home from the hospital he didn't check the hose. He just jumped in the car and we headed to the store again. We didn't make it because the car wasn't running right so he pulled over and raised the hood. The hose was missing.

He grabbed me by the hand and we headed back up the road. All the time he was cussing out my uncle. Finally I asked him why he was so upset and he said that idiot didn't tighten the clamps on the hoses. I knew right away what he meant.

"I said he didn't fix the car grand daddy I did."

He stopped dead in his tracks and looked down at me. He kneeled down so that we were face to face and said, "child are you telling me that you put that radiator hose on the car". I started crying and said yes grand daddy I did. I'm sorry, I thought I fixed it. I just wanted to surprise you. His eyes got all misty and he said well you did surprise me. I love you child.

He picked me up and carried me the rest of the way. Just before we got to the house we found the hose lying on the ground. We went to the house and got a gallon of water and went back to the truck. He handed me the hose and a screwdriver and with a smile on his face he said try again. I've had a wrench in my hand ever since.

"That's a great story. Hey Resa is that one over there?"

"Yes it is, hey it looks like it's in pretty good shape. Let's go check it out."

"Well…the nuts on the window hinge are rusted so we have to be very careful taking them off or we might burst the window. The good news is this car hasn't been out here that long. So the master cylinder should be in good working condition. I'm going to get the master cylinder."

"Resa; I can't afford the cylinder and the window too."

"Just leave that to me Rich. Give me the money and get in the car, I'll handle Charles."

"Rich can I drive back?"

"Well I guess but remember it's not a Honda."

"How can I forget, you keep telling me that? Rich sweetheart, is it ok, if we go pick up my things?"

"What things are you talking about?

My personal items, clothes and so on. Don't worry, it's on the way."

"Alright but we need to get back to the station soon."

"Can I ask you a question Rich?"

"Sure Resa…What is it?"

"The station is not doing that well is it?"

"No it's not."

"The owner is in the hospital, so how are you going to deal with any relatives that might show up and fire both of us?"

"That's a good question Resa, I've thought about that myself more than once. As far as I know he only has one relative as I've told you before. What I didn't tell you is I contacted someone who I thought was his daughter but she denies knowing him. She said her father died fifteen years ago."

"What makes you think she is his daughter?"

"I found her name and address on the back of a picture in his bedroom."

You went through his stuff?"

"I'm not proud of it but yes I did. He's my boss I thought I owed it to him to contact his family."

"Ok, I guess I can understand that. So what happens if he dies?"

"I don't know but let's hope that doesn't happen."

"Well I know you don't want that to happen but what if it does. Do you think you can just keep driving his car and running his station as if it were your own?"

"What's with all the questions?"

"I'm just saying, I think you should start thinking about these things. If we are going to go through all the trouble to open the garage and fix things up a bit, we should also prepare for the unexpected is all I'm saying."

"You talk with a lot of sense for someone who is only twenty four."

"Don't make fun of me. I grew up in this area and I know there are a lot of con artists out there and you had better be preparing yourself for them."

"I thought you said you were from South Jersey?"

"That is what I said."

"Resa sometimes you don't make a lot of sense but there is one thing that is working in our favor."

"What's that?"

"Well…no one knows he's in the hospital. I bet I could move into his house and live there and no one would be the wiser."

"Don't be so sure about that. What about the woman that you called in the middle of the night?"

"What about her?"

"Do you really think that she's put that phone call in the middle of the night out of her head?"

"She said she's not his daughter."

"You called her from his house didn't you?"

"Yes I did."

"I think you should call her again."

"Why should I do that?"

"Just to make sure she's out of the picture."

"What am I going to say to her?"

"Rich did you tell her which hospital he was in?"

"No, I didn't but it wouldn't be hard for her to find out if she wanted to."

"Rich you should call her again from his house but do it at a reasonable hour. Maybe she will have more to say this time."

"What if she sticks to her story?"

"Then I suggest that you get an attorney and try to get temporary ownership of the station or a least power of attorney to operate his affairs."

"I thought of that already and the risk is just too great. I figure I'll just run things like I've been doing and not raise any red flags. I really don't feel like being unemployed right now."

"Why are we stopping?"

"This is where I live."

"Do you need a hand?"

"No, I only have a few things, I won't be long."

As Rich waited for his mechanic, he wondered if he was doing the right thing. Would it really be so bad to just go back home? He would give this some serious thought tonight...

"You were right, that wasn't long. Is that everything?"

"Yes, I don't like to collect a lot of stuff. It makes it easier to relocate, plus I like to travel light."

"I see your point and I completely understand Resa. When we get to the station I think we should sit down and work out a schedule. I was thinking that we could share the duties during the day but alternate the hours at night."

"Are there enough customers to stay open all night?"

"Sometimes there are more at night than during the day."

"I think once you open that garage that's all going to change. I think staying open all night is a thing of the past Rich besides, I'm not much of a night person."

"Now you tell me....

Chapter 4

"You did a great job on the window. I can't tell it was ever broken."

"You got lucky this time Rich. Tomorrow I'll replace the Master Cylinder."

"What, we didn't buy the cylinder."

"I worked out something with Charles.

"Really and just what was that?"

Ding, ding…

"Sounds like we've got a customer."

"I'll get it Rich."

"Hello, how can I help you today?"

"I need to talk to a mechanic. My car keeps stalling."

"I'm a mechanic."

"Are you really?"

"Sure I am. Now how long has your car been stalling?"

"It started a couple of days ago. It normally happens when I come to a stop light."

"Sounds like you have a problem with your idle stabilizer bar. When is the last time you had a tune up?"

"It's been a while."

"We can tune it for you for about sixty buck and that includes parts and labor but you'll have to leave it for a couple of hours."

"You're going to fix my car?"

"Yes and we give a thirty day warranty."

"Alright but I'm headed to work. I'll have to pick it up later tonight."

"That will be fine, just leave me your number."

"Do you have a phone? I'll need to call a taxi."

"The phone is right this way Sir."

"Rich back the Chevy out of the garage; we got our first service repair."

"What are you talking about silly woman? We're not prepared for that."

"Keep your voice down before the customer hears you. Now pull the Chevy out and pull the gentleman's Buick into the bay."

"What's wrong with it?"

"It needs a tune up, "I think"."

"Come outside with me young lady. What are you doing? We don't have parts for a tune up."

"I know that but we will. Just trust me. Besides, how can we turn down a thirty dollar job? It doesn't get any simpler than a tune up."

"What about parts Resa?"

"You just leave that to me. I need the keys to the Chevy."

"Look we can't leave the station again today."

"We're not leaving, I am. I also need twenty dollars for the parts."

"Wait a minute. Twenty dollars for the parts, five dollars for gas, which only leaves a five dollar profit. Resa, it's almost not worth it."

"Relax Rich the twenty dollars for parts is not just for the Buick, it's for the next several cars that come in. We have to stock things like common belts, hoses, clamps, etc., that way we don't have to run to the junkyard every time we have a job."

"Are you sure you can do all of this with just twenty bucks?

"It will be a piece of cake my friend."

"Okay tell Charles that I said hi and please woman be careful with that car."

"I will Rich. Once again you're worrying about the wrong thing."

"What does that mean?"

"It means you need to give that lady in Tennessee another call."

"Ok, I'll call her now."

Mommy the phone is for you."

"Tell them to call back later honey."

"My mommy says please call back later."

"Please tell your mommy that this is an emergency."

"Mommy, he says it's an emergency."

"Hello...

"Hi, is this Elizabeth?

"Yes, this is she. Who is this?"

"My name is Rich. We spoke last week about your father."

"I told you that my father is dead! Why do you insist on calling me?"

"I'm sorry but he only has one daughter that I know of and there is no other family."

"Mister how did you get my number?"

"It was on the back of a picture I found at his home. It also had your name on it."

"Tell me about this picture."

"It's a picture of him, his wife and a little girl about ten years old. It was taken in front of his gas station where I work."

"Where is this gas station?"

"Ten miles east of Queens in a town called Hempstead."

"What is the little girl wearing?"

"She's wearing a white dress with a green tie around the middle."

"Oh my God! Is the lady in the picture wearing a blue dress with a scarf around her neck?"

"Yes, as a matter of fact, she does have a brown scarf around her neck. It is you…isn't it? Hello, hello…"

"No for the last time, it's not me. Don't ever call my home again! Have you got it! Never call my home again!"

Click...

After Elizabeth hung up the phone, she ran upstairs to the attic and opened a chest that hadn't been opened in over twelve years. With trembling hands she took out an old photo album. She opened it to the last page and stared at the picture of her mother, father and the little girl in the pretty white dress. They were standing in front of an old gas station with wide smiles on their face. They seemed so happy. On the back of the picture was the names Elizabeth, Harry and Lizzy.

"What is going on?" she screamed. I thought this was the only copy of this picture"

"Hey Rich do you think you can give me a hand with this?"

"Sure what do you need me to do?"

"I want you to get in the car and press the brake peddle all the way to the floor but don't do anything until I tell you."

"Don't take you foot off until I tell you."

"Okay, I think I can do that."

"I mean it Rich. Do not take your foot off the peddle until I say so."

"I heard you the first time boss lady."

"Ok Rich, press the brake peddle and hold it down."

"What exactly are we doing?"

"We are bleeding the brakes. Holding the peddle to the floor removes all the air out of the brake lines so that the brakes work properly. This is the old fashioned way but it works just fine...if it's done correctly."

"My leg is getting stiff. How much longer do I have to hold this freaking peddle down?"

"Until I say so, don't worry it's almost done."

"I have to say Resa, "it's been great having you around here." Since we opened the garage we are actually starting to make a profit at this place. That reminds me, I need to deposit this money into Mr. Sanford's account."

"That seems like a silly idea to me. Why don't you just put the money in a safe place for now? He's in a coma, there is no way a bank will let him withdraw any money in his condition...I want a raise Rich."

"Don't be crazy, you've only worked here two weeks." You might be right about the money though. Maybe I will put it in a safe place for now."

"Well good...you are finally using that head of yours for more than just a place to grow that hippie hair. Now back to my raise. You just said we are making money now."

"Lady...it's not our money and please clean those finger nails."

"I just cleaned them an hour ago. Rich, if old man Sanford dies; who gets the money then?"

"Shut your mouth woman, he's not going to die!"

"You might as well face it Rich, he's already dead. He's been in a coma for a month now. You can't locate his daughter. The way I see it, you are the closest thing that he has to family. So who gets the money when he dies Rich? I'll tell you who. You do Rich and do you want to know why?"

"Yes, "old mighty Teresa", please tell me why."

"It's as simple as the clouds in the sky idiot man. Without you this place wouldn't be making any money."

"Hey witch…don't you call me an idiot!"

"Okay, I was wrong for saying that. I'm sorry Rich; I don't know what gets into me sometimes."

"You can release the peddle now."

"Great, my leg was starting to get numb."

"Don't get out of the car yet. I need you to press the brakes and tell me how they feel."

"Ok, they feel a little strange."

"Do you mean spongy?"

"Yeah, I guess that's a good description."

"Ok, I need you to press the brake peddle one more time and hold it down. Press it hard Rich."

"Okay but the peddle just went straight to the floor."

"That's what it's supposed to do, just hold it there. Alright take your foot off them and press again."

"Now they seem hard."

"Try to push them to the floor."

"I'm trying but they won't go."

"Good Richie, my boy, I think we're done. Lets take her for a spin around the block."

"Let's go and let me know what happens when you press the brakes."

"Hey they're not pulling to the right anymore."

"That's great; now slam on them at the next stop sign."

"Okay, here we go. They still didn't pull to the right, I think you fixed them."

"It looks like I did. So when do I get a raise?"

"I'm afraid that's not going to happen. We should get back to the station."

"Hey Resa, it looks like we got company at the station."

"Who is that?"

"That's Sergeant Malloy, he's ok."

"Trust me Rich when I say; "ain't no cop ok." What do you think he wants?'

"He's probably checking up on Sanford's kin folk."

"Well you deal with him, I'm going upstairs and take a nap, wake me in one hour."

"Hello Rich. How are you doing?"

"I'm fine Sergeant. How are you?"

"I'm just fine. Any luck locating the daughter?"

"No, I'm afraid not."

"I was hoping that might be her in the car with you just now."

"No, that's my mechanic."

"Did you say your mechanic?"

"Yes I did and she's a good one."

"Oh I don't doubt that, I just didn't know the place had a mechanic that's all."

"Does old man Sanford know about all this?"

"Does he know about what?"

"You are driving his car, hiring new help and all."

"Well no, but that doesn't mean he won't approve besides, I know better than anyone what his plans are for this place and I mean to make sure we are right on track when he comes out of that dumb coma!"

"Easy Rich, no harm intended. Any luck with the next of kin?"

"I'm afraid not."

"No one has even called to say hi to the old fellow?"

"No they haven't. Sometimes family can be cold. I remember about ten years ago my family sort of let me down Sergeant."

"How do you mean Rich?"

"It's a crazy story but I guess I don't really blame them. It was a confusing time for me in my life. I had just gotten out of the Army. I was young and I thought I knew more about life than I really did. I had a family to support and I wasn't doing a good job of it. The truth of the matter was that the ARMY gig wasn't working and I decided to leave. The problem is you can't just leave the military because you don't agree with the way things are going.

My first four years were pretty good I had received an honorable discharge and was ready to get out. Then I found out my wife was pregnant so I reenlisted and things went down hill from there.

There were a lot of things that went wrong after that but the one thing that haunts me the most was the purse snatching incident.

"What was the purse snatching incident Rich?"

"Well Malloy, I had been out looking for work in a county close to home most of the day but I wasn't having any luck. It had gotten dark and I knew it was time to head home. I had about nine bucks in my pocket so I decided to go into the store and buy some milk, eggs and flour so that my family would have food for breakfast. Just as I was stepping out of the car I saw a young black guy snatch a purse from an elderly woman.

Without thinking I took off running after the guy. I chased him down the side walk and around the back of the store. I leaped at him and we both fell to the ground. He dropped the purse and jumped up and ran into the woods.

I picked the purse up and started walking back toward the store where the old couple was. Just as I came around the corner a crowd of people started pointing and yelling at me, saying there he is." I stopped dead in my tracks because I was afraid that they thought I was the one who took the purse.

When they got closer they started yelling at me to put down the purse. I quickly put the purse down and tried to explain that they had the wrong person but they didn't believe me.

I yelled to them that the guy who had taken the purse had just run into the woods but they weren't buying it. They had sticks and hammers and they told me not to move until the police got there.

Maybe I should have listened to them but I didn't. I ran and got in my car and headed home. Someone wrote down my license plates and the next day the police were at my home.

They took me to the police station and I tried to explain what had happened. They didn't even pretend to listen to me.

My wife at the time didn't believe me. She was so embarrassed that she threatened to abort the baby growing inside her for the last two months.

I was locked up in the county jail for a couple of months. No one came to visit me for the first seven weeks. Finally my parents came and bought me the news that one of my cousins had been killed in a car accident. A couple of weeks after that my father bailed me out of jailed. He and my mother slowly drove me away from the wonderful dark hole that I had known as my home for the past three months.

"It was a very quiet ride."

They dropped me off at my wife's house. She wasn't there and she didn't know I was out but I knew she wouldn't want me there. She had made no attempt to see me in over two months.

I can still remember the look on her face when she came into the house and saw me there. It was a very uncomfortable situation. She treated me like the criminal that I felt I was, even though I knew I was innocent I still felt guilty because I knew that's how people saw me

You would think that three months would be enough time served for snatching a purse, "if you actually did it." Unfortunately for me there had been a rash of purse snatching in the two county area and they were sure they had their man so they knew they had to make an example out of him. So what better way to send a message to everyone; send his Carolina country butt off to prison.

I'll make a very long story short Sergeant. They let me stay out of county jail long enough to be with my wife until my son was born. After that I was sent to the prison for bad boys where I spent another three months until someone realized that I wasn't the purse snatcher after all.

The Governor released me one day before Christmas. I signed papers that I would not sue the state and I was free...

My sister and my wife picked me up at the Greyhound Bus terminal and nothing about the past six months was discussed...ever."

"I'm sorry about that Rich. Didn't even know you had been married. Hey, what can I say. Sometimes we make mistakes. The system is not perfect. I'll be one of the first people to admit that but it's all we have. Is there anything that I can do to restore your faith in our judicial system?"

"Nothing Sergeant, I wish there was but there isn't. I lost my friends and a lot of my family during that time. The sad part is they will never know the truth and even if they did I'm not sure it would make a difference now. Sadly most people would rather believe the worst about you even when the truth is staring them straight in the face. It was shortly after that I started working on my art. I don't really need family or friends when I did that. Now if you'd kindly excuse me I have a couple of customers that need my attention."

"There's just one thing Rich. Do you know what's going to happen to this place if your boss dies and there isn't any next of kin to claim this place?"

"I don't know Sergeant; I just keep praying that he lives."

"Well my boy by law the city has the right to take over this place if he dies. You did know that didn't you?"

"No I didn't."

"It's something you should be thinking about. Normally when they do take over property they close it down and put up a chain length fence. I'd hate to see that happen to you and this place, so I strongly suggest you find his daughter or produce some type of documents that says you are to remain as the owner or something. I have to go now. I'll talk to you again real soon."

"Rich what's ailing you?"

"Oh it's nothing new; I just have a lot on my mind."

"He's right you know." That's the same darn thing that I told you last week. When are you going to start listening to somebody?"

"Do you know what this place needs Resa?"

"You're changing the subject again...

"It needs a fresh coat of paint on the outside."

"You got to be kidding me Rich. I didn't sign on here to be doing no crazy painting."

"I know you didn't." Don't worry, I'll do it myself."

"Rich paint is going to be expensive, especially enough to paint this dump."

"You just handle the customers for the next couple of days and I'll handle the painting."

"Whatever…you're the boss."

"There's just one more thing Resa."

"What is that?"

"I want you to make sure that every penny earned finds its way into the cash register."

"What are you saying?"

"I'm saying if someone buys ten dollars worth of gas then by golly there better be ten dollars going into the register. Room and board does not mean skimming off the profits. I'm going to Wal-Mart, I'll be back soon."

"Wal-Mart doesn't need your money Rich, go to one of the neighborhood mom and pop stores. That's if you can find one that

"Wally World" hasn't put out of business."

The Chevy was driving better than ever. Not only had my ace mechanic fixed the windows and brakes she had also tuned up the Chevy and it had made a world of a difference in the way it drove.

I liked Resa; I can only imagine the state of the garage without her. She's a good kid and I liked having her around. I had hoped that she'd stop stealing money though but it had gotten a little out of hand. I know she's not going to stop but maybe she'll be a little more discreet about it.

I took her advice and got the paint from a small store just a few blocks from the station. It was more expensive than buying it from Wally-

World but it was the principal that mattered and she was right about that bit of advice.

She was also right about finding Mr. Sanford's relatives. I got him some fresh flowers and dropped them off at the nurse's station. I didn't even bother to ask how he was or if I could see him. The one thing that I was sure about was the fact that he would come out of the coma. It wasn't a matter of if but when.

Painting was my passion, even though it was a different type of painting it was painting none the less. I started late on Thursday and by Saturday afternoon it was finished. I painted the building maroon and the trim white. "It was a master piece."

The few regular customers complimented me on the new paint job, even Resa appeared impressed. The only thing that stood out like a sore thumb around the place now were those old, rusty, nineteen fifty pumps. I considered painting them but no amount of paint would improve their appearance.

"Well Rich; I have to admit the place is starting to look great. Where are those painting of yours?"

"Why do you ask?"

"I have an idea. You didn't toss them away did you?"

"No I didn't."

"Well where are they?"

"They're out back in the shed."

"Can I look at them?"

"Sure I guess. Why the sudden interest in them Resa?"

"I think you should display them Rich."

"Display them where?"

"Here at the station. You can hang them on the walls. You've spruced up the place outside.

Lets see what those pictures can do for the inside."

"They are not meant to be hung up in a place like this."

"Oh really...and I guess being tossed away inside that shed is a better place."

"Ok Resa...let's go get them. We have to be careful how we handle them. They are all on canvas and can rip very easy. If that happens they are ruined."

"How many do you have?"

"There are about twenty left I think."

"How many did you have?"

"There was a total of twenty seven."

"So you did sell some painting."

"No, I gave them away. They were portraits of my sisters and Karen my ex-girlfriend."

"You never mentioned a girlfriend. Tell me about her.

"Not much to tell really, except she dumped me once I moved here."

"Why didn't she come with you?"

"She wanted no part of the big city life. She asked me to come back a few weeks after I moved here but I said no. The truth of the matter was I was too embarrassed to go back. We lived in a small town with people who had small dreams. It was kind of a big deal to everyone when I decided to come here and make a living selling my art. Everyone would have really gotten a kick out of me high tailing it back there after just two weeks. Most of them think I'm up here living the life of a rich artist somewhere in Manhattan."

"Now Rich, where would they get an idea like that?"

"Don't ask Resa."

"Do you stay in touch with Karen?

"No, I'm afraid not she ran off and got herself hitched several months after I moved here. It didn't work out for her though."

"Do you plan on getting back with her?"

"Nope, she said I was an idiot, with idiot dreams. I haven't heard from her since."

"You're not an idiot Rich."

"Thank you for saying that."

"Here's my art."

"Can I take this one outside and unwrap it."

"Sure but be careful with it Resa. Like I said before they are very delicate."

"Wow…this is a nice picture Rich. Are you sure you painted this?"

"Yes and don't act so surprised."

"I ain't acting fool. I am surprised. I can't believe no one would buy this. Are the others this good?"

"Well...yeah, I guess they are."

"I can't wait to see them. Rich bring this picture and come into the station with me."

"They are not pictures Resa. They are called art."

"Well...they look like pictures to me. The walls inside the station can be your art gallery. Anyone that comes in the store will be able to see them. Heck plenty of people come in here. You never know someone might see something that they like. You might even sell one of them."

"I don't think Mr. Sanford would approve of that Resa."

"You can worry about that if and when he comes out of that coma."

"I don't know…it just doesn't seem right."

"Come on man; you practically own the place. You invited yourself into his house. You're driving his car all up and down Southern State Parkway and you're worried about hanging a few pictures."

"Let's do it but first, I think I should paint the walls in here."

"No, no, the walls need that rugged look. It will set off your painting better if you leave it like it is."

"Well okay but I at least need to wash the walls."

"Okay you start removing the old things and wash the walls if you must, "crazy man." While you're doing that, "I'll bring in the other painting." Oops…I mean other "art" in."

Chapter 5

"Herman I got a call today. One of my relatives from New Jersey died."

"Oh honey, I'm sorry to hear that. Who was it?"

"It was just a third or fourth cousin. Kind of don't make them family at all they're so distant."

"Lizzy, I can't believe you of all people said that. Family is family down to the last limb on the tree."

"Of course you're right Herman. I'm afraid that I need to catch a plane today."

"You can't wait until tomorrow?"

"No, I'm afraid not, the funeral is tomorrow. I need to catch a plane in the next couple of hours."

"Do you want me to go with you?"

"No, you have work and Elizabeth has school. I'll be back the day after tomorrow."

"Okay but this is a little weird Liz."

"Don't worry honey. I'm just glad someone called me in time. I'll call you when I get there. I love you….bye for now."

Elizabeth packed a small bag and placed the picture in her purse. She hated to lie to her husband but he just wouldn't understand.

"Rich this one is the most beautiful one of all. Can I put this one in my room upstairs?"

"You like that one?"

"Yes, "it's so nice." I could stare at it all day."

"All day huh…well in that case you can have it."

"Oh, I love it! Thank you so much Rich. I can't believe you have this kind of talent. Why you haven't sold one of these is a mystery to me. Why I'd give you fifty dollars for any one of them."

"Thanks Resa. You are so generous. The one in your hand there should sell for about ten thousand dollars."

"Come on Rich, you're kidding me right."

"No I'm not. Each of these should sell for at least that price and more."

"Who in their right mind would pay that much for a painting?"

"First of all they are not paintings, they are art. Take the one that you have in your hand. If that "painting" as you call it were put on display by a famous artist, it would sell for one hundred thousand dollars easy." It's all about the name Resa and if the famous artist is dead that same picture would go for at least twice that amount."

"Well don't go getting yourself famous Rich, I don't want to be tempted to kill you and collect on all these painting."

"That's pretty good (ha, ha). I'll keep that in mind. When we finish hanging this art, let's get some dinner. After that, I'm going to make a trip to Mr. Sanford's home."

"Can I go?"

"What about the station?"

"Can I go?..."

"Alright but let's do it now, we can grab something to eat on the way."

"Can I drive?"

"You are just full of questions aren't you? I guess so. What do you want to eat?"

"I'll eat anything except that dang Chinese that you've been feeding me the last couple of days."

"I thought you liked Chinese."

"I do but not every day of the freaking week. I'm starting to feel like I'm only four feet tall.

Besides, have you ever seen a Chinese eat any of that food?"

"Sure I have."

"Think about it Rich, I've been to a lot of different Chinese places and the only thing I ever see them eating is the rice."

"That's true; I have to agree with you. Okay, we'll go somewhere and get some real food. Let's go over to 39th and Edmire. There's a great restaurant over there."

"Now that was a good meal."

"Yes it was Rich but wouldn't you hate to be a chicken."

"Oh now I guess you are going to complain about Soul food."

"No that stuff was great. We could have that seven days a week and I wouldn't complain. It's just too bad that it will eventually kill you."

"There is just no pleasing you…is there?"

"Rich, I can't remember the last time a man pleased me."

"Oh crap Resa; I think you are on a totally different subject now. I think you better just sit back and enjoy the ride to Mr. Sanford's house. We'll be there in less than fifteen minutes."

"So this is where your boss lives."

"Yes this is his home."

"Are you sure we should go in?"

"I've already been in there once, so one more time isn't going to hurt."

"I don't know Rich, it just seems kind of wrong."

"I'm his employee and I have to look after his affairs for him."

"I know it's wrong but it's necessary. I'm just glad there's someone with me this time."

"Why do you say that?

"Let's just say this place was a little spooky that night."

"How do you mean?"

"You wouldn't understand besides, maybe it was just me, I was tired and needed some rest. We'll talk about it later. Come on."

"Do we know what we are looking for?"

"We need to find papers or old mail with an address that could be his daughter's."

"We need to go through his mail. Isn't that a Federal offense?"

"Yes it normally would be considered a Federal Offense, however, I'm acting on Mr. Sanford's' behave and that makes it ok."

"If you say so but I don't think there's a Judge in the country that will buy that explanation. Rich I'm too young to be going to jail."

"So am I Resa. Just don't touch anything and I'll tell the Judge that you tried to talk me out of it."

"Ha, ha, you; Richie, are a funny, funny man."

"The name is Rich; now let's go into the den first, it's this way. Wait a minute. I locked this door when I left, I'm sure of it. I locked all the doors. Someone has been in here. Lets go upstairs. I need to get his chest. It's not here. I put it back in the closet, where I found it."

"Are you sure you put it back?"

"Resa, please stop saying that! I know what I did. Who could have taken it? The place was locked and it doesn't look like it was broken into. That can only mean one thing, someone has a key. Lets just think about this for a moment."

"Maybe, he has a girlfriend."

"He didn't have a girlfriend. I would have known."

"Lets go Rich. I'm getting scared. How do we know someone's not in here right now."

"We can't leave yet. Be quiet for a second will you! The night that I was here I felt like some-one was in the house when I got here. Whoever or whatever it was nearly gave me a heart attack. I'm afraid that if we don't find the information that we need this time we won't be able to re-turn to this house."

"What about his mailbox?"

"That's a good idea little lady, lets go check it. It's just outside the door."

"It looks like someone beat us to it. The mail box is completely empty."

"His mail is gone and the chest is gone. Someone is searching for the same information that we are. We won't find what we are looking for in this house. We're too late. Lets head back to the station I have an idea."

"Wait Rich. Before we do that, lets check the bathroom."

"Resa, you just might be the smartest person I ever met. You go check his shower."

"It's dry Rich and so is the soap. The wash rags are all dry and the toilet needs to be flushed. No one has been in here for a long time."

"Well another dead end but it was a great idea."

"I have one more."

"Go ahead I can't wait to hear it."

"Lets go talk to the neighbors."

"No little lady; we can't do that."

"Come on Rich maybe they saw someone over here."

"You mean like they might be watching us right now? Let's go, I think have an idea."

"Mister Newell where are we going? This isn't the way back to the station."

"How's your acting skills Resa?"

"What acting skills? Man what are you talking about?"

"You wanted to hear my idea...well here it is. We are going to the hospital Elizabeth."

"Who is Elizabeth?"

"Why you are my dear and you can't wait to see your father, Mr. Harold Sanford. I think you can summon up some tears can't you?"

"You want me to pretend to be his daughter?"

"That's one of the things I like about you Elizabeth. You catch on quick."

"I won't do it, I can't do it! Ain't nobody going to believe that I'm his estranged daughter!"

"Sure they will. No one here has ever seen her and besides, who would suspect foul play. You are just a distraught daughter who just learned her father is in a coma."

"Rich please don't ask me to do this. I'll never be able to pull it off besides, I don't see the point."

"The point is I need to know that he is indeed in a coma. I also need to know if anyone has been to see him."

"I thought you said that only family could see him."

"That's true, only family can go in his room but someone could have brought him flowers or a get well card. The only way to find out is for you to get inside his room and look around."

"Rich, I'll need something to drink first."

"What?"

"You heard me! I'll need something to drink first."

"Alright but don't over do it."

"Turn right at the second light. There's a liquor store not too far from here."

"How do you know that?"

"Please give me a break boss, you've lived here two years and you don't know where anything is around here do you."

"Resa; you go inside. I'll wait out here for you."

"Over my dead, cold body you will. Don't you think it will be more believable if you are with me? They have seen you at least half a dozen times. It only makes sense that you would come to the hospital with me when I got to town."

"Okay, that makes sense now lets go."

"Wait, I just need one more small sip."

"No Resa! They'll be able to smell the alcohol on your breath." "Now lets go!

"Hello, I'm here to see my father. His name is Harold Sanford."

"Wait one moment miss, I'll be right back."

"She doesn't believe me lets go."

"Miss your father is in room 429. It's about time someone came to see him."

I just found out."

"Alright but you can only stay a few minutes."

"How is he?"

"I'm afraid there hasn't been any change. You just never know about these things. I've seen people stay in a coma for years and others just a matter of days. Some come out of it and walk right out of here like there was never a thing wrong with them. Others I'm afraid are never the same. Your father is a fighter, I can tell you that."

"Can my friend come in with me?"

"No I'm sorry, family only."

"It's okay Miss Sanford, "I'll wait for you in the lobby."

"Thank you Richie."

Resa's hands trembled as she entered the cold dark room. There were no windows. The room felt more like a prison than a hospital. She wanted to turn and run from the tomb like room but instead she said.

"Hello dad. How are you? I'm sorry it took me so long to get here but I just found out this morning. I know you probably can't hear me but I want you to know I love you."

"This room feels so empty. Dad, I'll bring you some flowers when I come back. Nurse what is this machine?"

"It monitors your father's brain activity. See these lines on the monitor. As long as lines are present we know your father has a chance of recovery. If the activity decreases then we start to worry."

"I'm sorry but I'm going to ask that you leave now."

"I understand, Dad I don't know if you can hear me but remember how much I love you."

"It's alright, if you kiss him before you leave."

"Yes nurse that will be a great idea."

"I love you Dad. Please don't leave me, "I love you so, so much." I'll be back soon."

"Nurse I can't stand (sob) to see him like that. How could this happen?"

"Be strong Miss Sanford and pray. That's the only thing that can help right now. We will make sure he's comfortable. I'm afraid that's the only thing we can do."

"I know you are doing your best but it's so hard to see him like that. He has always been so full of energy, so (sob) full of life. I have to go now."

"Well...Resa what did you see?"

"I saw an old man with a lot of wires coming out of his head. Don't ask me to go back there. His room smells like death."

"Were there any signs that someone might have been visiting him?"

"I saw no signs of anyone being there. I did notice a picture though. They had it suspended from the ceiling with a string right in front of his face."

"That's the picture that I found in his house. I think it's his daughter and deceased wife. Can you imagine what must be going through his mind?"

"What do you mean Rich?"

"I mean the picture. If he is able to understand anything, he'll be wondering how that picture got out of his home and into his hospital room."

"Rich, that's not the only thing he'll be wondering about. He'll also be trying to figure out why his daughter has changed so much since he last saw her."

"That's also true Resa. Yes, that is very true."

Chapter 6

Honey, I just landed in Newark, New Jersey."

"Great how was your flight?"

"It was fine. I'm heading to pick up my rental car now."

"What you getting?"

"Well…I reserved a Ford Taurus but you can never tell about these rental places. They normally give you whatever they want you to have. Sometimes I wonder what the word reserve really means."

"Bring me and Lizzy back a slice of the Big Apple."

"I hadn't planned to go into New York but if you want something, I guess I could. I've got another call coming through honey. I'll call you later."

"Hello, my name is Elizabeth Elkhart. I reserved a Ford Taurus."

"May I see your driver license and credit card please? Yes…Mrs. Elkhart we have a black Taurus for you. It's parked in stall 373. The tank is full of gas and it's ready to go. Is there anything else we can do for you?"

"Thank you but that will be all."

"Enjoy your Taurus and thanks for renting from Hertz."

"Hello my name is Lisa. Can you look at my car? It keeps overheating when I stop at a light or a stop sign but when I start driving again it seems to cool down."

"Sure pull into the garage and I'll take a look at it. Are you in a hurry?"

"Sort of but I have some time."

"Here have a soda, it's on the house. You can have a seat inside and I'll check out your car."

"You're the mechanic?"

"Yes I am and if I had a penny for each time I've been asked that this week...

"I'm sorry you just look far too pretty to be a mechanic. All you need is a dress and you could enter the beauty pageant right now. Your eyes are so beautiful and mysterious."

"Thank you Lisa, that's a very kind thing to say but I haven't worn a dress in a very long time. Now go have a seat, I'll be right back."
"Thanks for the soda...

"Lisa, it looks like your water pump is out. We can fix that for you for about eighty bucks."

"How long will it take?"

"I can have it ready for you first thing to-morrow morning."

"Alright but I'm not paying more than eighty dollars. I've been ripped off more times than I care to remember."

"I understand, "you don't have to worry about that here." There is one other thing Lisa and it's completely up to you."

What is it?"

"I strongly recommend replacing the timing belt. I can get you one for about twenty dollars. I won't charge you extra because I have to remove the old to replace the water pump anyway. If we don't change it and that belt goes, "you'll be out of more than just a hundred bucks."

"Alright but that's all I can afford."

"How far away do you live?"

"I'm about eight miles away. I'll just call a taxi."

"No need for that, we can give you a ride. Here have a seat and another soda, "it's also on the house." Just give me five minutes and we can be on our way."

"Rich I need to make a run out to the junk-yard."

"What for this time?"

"I need to pick up a water pump and a timing belt. There are also a few other things I should try to get while I'm up there."

"Are you going to fix her car with parts from the junk yard?"

"Sure, there are a lot of good parts out there."

"Alright, how much is this going to cost me?"

"We get seventy-five dollars for a water pump job right. I can get a used one for ten bucks but to be on the safe side I'll get two and there you have it a fifty dollar profit."

"I think that would be a fifty-five dollar profit Resa."

"No Rich you're forgetting about the five dollars worth of gas to get there and back."

"So how much you need?"

"Thirty should cover it and I'll return all change. We got to find a way to get some inventory on hand so we don't have to run to the junk yard every time we need to fix a car."

"That's going to be a tough order to fill little lady. There's no way for us to know which part these cars will need before they get here."

"Rich, all I'm saying, is we need a better plan that's all. I'll be back in a couple of hours. You can handle things until I get back right."

"Ha, ha, Resa; you are becoming quite the comedian."

"Howdy Charles...

"Hey there Reesa."

"It's Resa...Charles. I need this list of parts ready for me the next time I come out here. Can you handle this?"

"Let me look over the list."

"I'd pull them myself but I got to get back to the station."

"This is a big list but I'll get those parts for ya."

"Thank you."

"Resa, there's a great movie playing at the drive in. You want to go with me this weekend?"

"Maybe...what's playing?"

"I'm not sure but it's the drive in, "they always have good movies."

"Really...when was the last time you were at the drive in?"

"I went last weekend."

"Oh really...who was the lucky girl?"

"There was no girl. I went alone...like I always do."

"Oh my...that's so sad Charles. Here's the number to the station, give me a call in a couple of days and I'll let you know if I'm free. Now I need to go pull a couple of water pumps."

"Make sure you spin them before you take them off. It'll save you a lot of time in the long run."

"I ain't no amateur Charles."

"I'm back Rich."

"Great that didn't take too long."

"Well I got lucky with the traffic. You want to learn how to change a water pump."

"I need to watch the pumps Resa."

"Come on if anyone comes we'll hear them."

"I didn't hear you that day you came walking in here."

"That was different."

"How was it?"

"I didn't want to be heard. Just come give me a hand. You just might learn something. Besides, this is a simple job on this car. All water pump jobs are not so simple. You are a good painter but it's not putting any food on the table."

"It's not painting Resa...for the last time it's art."

"Whatever Rich, art...or fart, "it's still not putting any food on the table. You need to learn yourself a new trade and you got the best teacher around. Come on, I want to get this job done before night fall."

"What can I do?"

"For starters, get me that bucket over there. We'll use it to drain the antifreeze. Then get down here on the ground with me so I can show you a couple of things."

"The last time a woman wanted to show me a couple of things it almost cost me twenty bucks."

"Rich...it would cost you a heck of a lot more than that to see a couple of anything I got. Now mister, it's time to get serious and I hope you're not afraid to get your hands dirty. First thing we need to do is find the drain plug. That looks like it over there. Normally you can turn it with you hands but sometimes you have to use a wrench. Give it a turn to the left and lets see what happens. Make sure you have the bucket directly under it."

"It's not moving."

"Try a little harder."

"It's not moving, I tell you."

"Move over man and let me try. You got to use those muscles of yours Mr. Rich. There it goes, no wonder that girl back in Carolina left you. It was a little snug but I got it. Once it completely drains, we have to make sure we tighten it back. For that I normally use the wrench."

Ding, ding...

"You are saved by the bell again Rich. We have a customer. Don't take too long I don't want you to miss the good part."

"Don't you worry Resa. I can't wait to get back."

"Good evening Sir. How may I help you?

"Filler up and check the oil for me."

"Okay, this is a nice Cadillac. It must have cost a fortune."

"No it's a hand me down from my grandmother. Bless her soul. She left it to me when she went on to glory."

"Oh, I'm sorry to hear that."

"It's Okay mister. She was ninety something. She never did tell anyone her correct age."

"That'll be seventeen dollars."

"Here you go. Do you have a bathroom that I could use?"

"Sure do, follow me."

"I just love these old gas stations. Wait a minute. Who painted these? They are pretty good. Do you mind if I look around a bit."

"No, I don't mind but I thought you needed to use the bathroom."

"My friend the bathroom can wait, I must first allow my eyes to feast upon this fine art."

"You mean at the painting."

"Son these aren't painting, this is art, well almost art. The person that painted these is very talented. The artist just needs to accentuate more."

"What does that mean?"

"It's really hard to explain and even harder to accomplish. I'd like to meet the person who did these."

"You're looking at him."

"You painted these?"

"Yes I did most of these several years ago. I haven't done any new ones in over a year though."

"Why not son?"

"I lost interest."

"Do you mind if I send a colleague of mine to look at these?"

"No, I don't mind at all."

"Let me warn you; he's very critical but he might be able to guide you in the right direction. Are any of them for sale?"

"They all are Sir."

"Fantastic, I'll be in touch with you later. You have a good day, wait...can you point me toward that bathroom now?"

"Sure just follow me."

"Well Rich, it looks like someone might be selling one of those pictures soon. After we finish this job I think we should go out and celebrate."

"You heard what he said?"

"Yes I did, "congratulations Mr. Artist. Now are we going to fix this water pump or not?"

"Good evening Sergeant Malloy. What brings you to our side of town?"

"Hi Henry, I was hoping that you could help me with a cold case."

"Sure I'll try. Which one is it?"

"Remember the double murder at the Gas Station over on Clover and 19th street."

"Yeah, the police never did solve that one. Even though we all believed it was the owner. Who can blame a man when he comes home from a hard days work and finds his wife doing the hired help?"

"I agree that has to be a tough one Henry but I'm really more concerned with what happened to the daughter. No one seems to be able to locate her."

"Now why someone would be looking for her is a mystery to me?"

"Everything is a mystery to you. Can you get me that file?"

"Maybe but it'll take me a few hours. The case is so old that it's not in the Computer. I'll have to go through the files in the basement."

"Thanks Henry and I'd appreciate it if you wouldn't mention this to anyone."

"Sure thing Malloy but can I ask you a question?"

"Sure I guess. What's the question?"

"What would you have done if you had walked in on your old lady doing another man?"

"Probably the same as any other man Henry."

"I see...well give me a couple of hours and I'll dig through the files and see what I can come up with."

"I have a better idea Henry. Why don't I just go down there and look around myself."

"We both know that's not proper procedure Malloy."

"I realize that but this case is keeping me up at night. If I don't get my hands on that information soon, "I'll go crazy."

"Alright, even though this is not your jurisdiction, I'll allow it but if there is a problem of any kind that arises because of what you find in them there files, I'm completely ignorant of how you got your hands on the information. Is that understood?"

"Yes Henry, it's completely understood."

"One more thing Malloy, you can't take anything with you."

"I understand Henry."

"Here sign the book before you down."

"You going to make me sign the book Henry?"

"Everyone signs the book on my watch or they don't go down."

"Alright, where do l sign?"

"Right here and don't forget to sign out before you leave."

"Good afternoon Sir, how may I help you?'

"I'm looking for a Mr. Rich."

"He is inside the station."

"Good please fill her up and check the oil for me."

"Not a problem," said Resa.

"Hello, are you Mr. Rich?"

"Yes I am. What can I do for you?"

"My name is Douglas Brite. I'm with North-storm Art Gallery in Manhattan. An acquaintance asked me to look at your work."

"Great, I had almost given up on you. It's been almost two weeks since your friend was here."

"Is that the art hanging on the walls?"

"Yes, that's them."

"I see....give me a few minutes to look around."

"Take your time. Would you like a soda? It's on the house.

"No thanks, I don't drink sodas."

"Rich my boy...I'm afraid that I don't see any art. These are okay if you just want something to hang on the walls of your home but they all seem to be missing the artist's emotional state when he did the work."

"What do you mean?"

"Well when you painted this particular piece here, what was going on in your life? Was it a happy time or was it a sad time? Were you involved in a relationship that was blossoming or were you and your lover, if there was a lover just going through the motions?"

"That's a pretty loaded question but I would say things were ok at that time."

"Well there you have it. Most of our famous Artists were going through something when their paintings were captured. This is what's known as the, "window into the artist soul." It's here on the canvas that they allow us to understand them. I must be blunt with you Mr. Rich. Unless you change your technique you will never be able to aspire to that level."

"Are you saying that my art is trash?"

"No they are definitely not trash but they are not art either I'm afraid. Unfortunately, they are just pictures. There are millions of people out there painting pictures just like these. If I were you, I'd have a garage sale. Try to get twenty-five dollars for each of them. Now I must be going."

"I can't say that I'm unhappy to hear you say that."

"Do I sense a hint of disappointment in your voice Rich?"

"What you're sensing is not disappointment!"

"Would you rather I had lied to you about your pictures? I think not."

"Well did you come here to scorn me or to help?"

"It's not my job to help Rich. I simply look for talent and I'm afraid this is not talent."

"Well thanks for your advice, you may leave now."

"My last piece of advice to you is this. If you want to create art, look deep down inside of yourself. If you have what it takes, that's where you'll find it. Otherwise you'll be at this gas station for the rest of your life. Good day Mr. Rich by the way your sign said a free coke with a fill up."

"I thought you just said that you don't drink sodas."

"I don't but my grand kids do. I'll give it to one of them."

"Here's your coke Mr. Brite. Please have a good day."

"You were right Tim. I just looked at his art. He has talent. I think this guy can make us some money, if he's pointed in the right direction. Send Leo over at the end of the week to sign this guy up."

"How much are we going to invest in him?

"We should be able to get him for the minimum."

"Ok Doug, I'm on it."

Chapter 7

"Rich it has really been a slow day."

"Yes I know Resa. Why don't you take some time off? You can call your friend from the junk-yard and take him up on his offer."

"No thanks, I'm not interested in him. He'll just fall in love with me and I'll just end up breaking his heart. Isn't that what your girlfriend did to you?"

"Resa are you talking about Karen?"

"I can tell there is an empty place in your heart Rich. Why don't you try to get back with her?"

"You are right about the empty place in my heart. However, Karen didn't put it there."

"Well...if she didn't who did?"

"It's a long story Resa. It's a very, very long story."

"I want to hear the story Rich. We've got time."

"It's not that easy to talk about Resa."

"Come on Rich. We are friends. Maybe if you talk about it, you will feel better."

"It's a long story Resa. It goes back to my military days."

"I didn't know you were in the military."

"Well I was but the military wasn't in me."

"Please Rich...I really want to hear this story."

"Ok Resa, I'll make a deal with you. I'll tell you the story but only if you promise not to interrupt."

"I promise."

"I mean it Resa not one interruption during the entire story and it is indeed a long story."

"I said I promise Rich, so start talking."

In my neighborhood when I was growing up, it seemed everyone I knew had lived there his or her entire life. The married people had meet here, most went to the same school had been dating since high school, married at an early age and seemed to stay married forever. It was obvious that some were not happy ones. I was sure from what I had been taught since I was a kid that God wanted marriage to last. I often asked myself, "is this all there is to life? How can you be sure you are marrying the right person if you didn't see more of the world and meet more people?

I promised myself that this was not going to happen to me. I'll do some traveling when I graduated from high school. I would join the military? What better way to see the world, this decision could help me accomplish several things. They would help with my tuition for college. I could see the world save money and met lots of different women. I would not get married until I was around 35 years old.

I figured by then I would have graduated from medical school. I'd have a nice home, one that's far away from South Carolina. Yep, at the age of seventeen I had it all figured out.

Here's the problem with making plans. You have to prepare for the unexpected. If you don't you are leaving everything in the hands of fate and trust me when I say fate can sometimes play a nasty little trick on you.

I was so sure about what I wanted to do after I graduated that I enlisted in the military six months before I graduate from high school. I was ready to get on with the rest of my life. What I didn't realize was a month later a college would offer me a full scholarship to play football for them. I tried to get out of my military commitment but it was a lost cause. So, I headed off to the Army with a bitter taste in my mouth and for the first four months it wouldn't get much better.

I 'm sure you have heard the Army slogan, "Be All You Can Be". It sounds good doesn't it? Well let me tell you, there must be some kind of typo in that slogan. It should read, "Be All We Let You Be" which isn't much out side of your normal job. My dream of attending college while in the military quickly went up in smoke. For the next four years I'd have to be content with being, "all they let me be".

While most soldiers were out in the clubs I was stuck in a corner at the back of the library studying Anatomy for hours. This had become a ritual of mine for about six months.

One day when I came in someone was sitting at the desk I normally used. It would be the first time since I started going there that I had to sit at a different desk.

I found another desk and tried to study but I couldn't concentrate, so I decided to leave early. I found a book that I liked and approached the check out desk. As I was approaching the check out desk I noticed this cute girl behind the desk, "our eyes met and she quickly looked away." I had never seen her there before. I placed my book on the desk hoping to say a few words to her when out of nowhere the old librarian appeared.

"May I help you young man she whispered?"

"Yes, I whispered, I'd like to check out this book."

What I really wanted to say was…can I check out your little helper? When I turned around the cute girl had disappeared.

It would be three weeks before I would see her again. I was on my way into the library and she was rushing down the steps. She tripped and fell, books went everywhere. There must have been twenty of them." I rushed to her side to see if she was alright.

My first thought was where is she going with all those books anyway? My second thought was, wow, what a beautiful young lady. She had great legs and was wearing a short dress. I couldn't help but stare at her thighs they looked so good.

I asked her if she was ok but I guess I had stared at her beautiful legs a little too long because her only comment was I hope you got a good look! I tried to help her get off the ground but she pulled away from me and screamed...I'm just fine and I don't need your help!

"What's the big rush?" I asked.

"I was trying to catch that taxi," she said.

"Don't worry. There will be another one in about twenty minutes.

"I'm late already!" she snapped.

After I helped her pick up her books, I finally introduced myself. She looked at me as though she didn't understand English and looked at my hand as if it was a dirty foreign object. I quickly put it back in my pocket.

"Are you always this mean to people who try to help you?"

"Just the ones who stare at me like you were doing. That look only means one thing and I'm not the one mister, I am not the one!"

Despite her obvious annoyance with me she allowed me to stay there and hold her books until the next taxi came. I guess the bruises on her leg and arms hurt more than she let on. When she was safely inside the taxi I said you should get a doctor to look at that bruise on your thigh as soon as possible. I think it's been looked at enough for one day she said as she slammed the door.

I went to the library every chance I got for the next six weeks. I kept finding reasons to ask her questions. Strangely, one day out of the blue she approached my desk and said.

"Excuse me I hate to interrupt your studying but a friend of mine was asking about you the other day. If you'll walk me home I'll tell you what she had to say."

"I'd be glad to walk you home."

"Ok let's go."

"My friend asked me to find out if you were seeing anyone."

"She did?"

"Yes but I told her that the only thing you were seeing was those books of yours."

"How do you know that?"

"Well let's see, you've been coming to the library for at least nine months, right."

"Yes but how do you know that?"

"Rich, I've been working there almost two years and I notice things. For example: you always go to the same desk in the back of the library and you hardly moved for hours."

"I can't believe you've been here that long and I never saw you until a few months ago."

"Oh Rich, I think you saw me. You just never noticed me because you never look up from those books. What's in those books anyway? Maybe a treasure map."

"As a matter of fact, it is something like that."

"So are you interested in meeting my girl-friend?"

"I don't know, tell me about her."

"Well…she's very cute."

"Yeah right and I bet she has a great personality too, right."

"As a matter of fact she does."

"Well, I'm not into blind dates. I did that once and I promised myself I'd never do it again. She's probably a nice girl but I'm interested in someone else right now."

"You probably wouldn't have time to see her anyway. You are always in the library and when you are not there, you are somewhere playing soldier."

"You seem to know a lot about me. What you don't seem to know however is who I'm really interested in. Well my little librarian friend, let me give you a hint. A few months ago the most beautiful girl I had ever seen was running down the steps coming out of the library. This beautiful girl tripped and fell. I rushed over to help her. She had a bruise on her leg and I guess I stared at it too long. She was pretty nasty to me that day but I knew at that moment that I wanted her. You probably think I'm crazy after the way she treated me, but she is the only person I'm interested in right now and before I even think about anyone else I have to explore my options with her."

"What would you say to her to get her to give you a chance?"

"I don't know I'm still praying for the answer to that question."

"Well, you just continue to pray Rich. God always answers prayers. Just remember the answer you receive may not be the answer you want."

"I'll remember that."

"How many brothers and sisters do you have Aecia?"

"None, I'm an only child."

"Really...so is it true what they say about only children?"

"I'm not sure. What do they say?"

"I don't think you want to know."

"How many brothers and sisters do you have Rich?"

"I have two brothers and six sisters."

"Wow, you come from a big family."

Yes, "they're pretty cool for country folks."

"Is it true what they say about big families?"

"I'm not sure. What do they say about big families?"

"You know that everyone sleeps in the same bed and eats out of the same plate."

"What, I never heard that!"

"Me either, gotcha, ha ha. That's for trying to call me a spoiled brat earlier."

"Ok, I guess I deserved that."

"So why did you join the Army? I might be wrong but you seem too intelligent to be jumping from good airplanes."

"Well...it's like this Aecia. I have this dream of seeing the world, saving lots of money and meeting lots of pretty women."

"That's your dream Rich?"

"Yes it is."

"So how much of your dream has been accomplished so far?"

"Well, let me see. I've been in the Army 14 months. I've saved about sixty percent of the money I've made. I've been to Panama, North Carolina, Georgia and now Kentucky but I really haven't had time to go out and work on the meeting pretty women part.

"Why does it have to be a pretty woman? Shouldn't the kind of person she is matter."

"Oh it matters a lot but it also helps if she's pretty."

"Why are you men so hung up on looks? One of these days I hope you meet someone who isn't so pretty and you fall in love with her. That will serve you right Rich."

"Maybe someday that will happen but today, all I see is a pretty woman who won't give me the time of day."

"Who are you talking about?"

"I'm talking about Aecia."

"You think I'm pretty Rich?"

"Yes I do." I thought that from the very first day I saw you."

"Thank you. That's a very nice thing for you to say."

"So are you going to give me a chance or not?"

"Why should I? All men are the same and only after one thing anyway. I don't know why the face on it has to be pretty."

"First of all, it's not the same and secondly everyone wants someone that looks good."

"I'll never see your point Rich but there will come a day when you will see mine."

"How old are you Aecia?"

"That's none of your business Richie."

"Please don't call me Richie. You sound like an old woman Aecia you need to loosen up a little."

"If you must know, I'm twenty and I was right about you. I think my friend is better off without you. I'm so glad we had a chance to talk. I'll tell her that she should forget about you."

"What's her name Aecia?"

"Why do you need to know that?"

"I want to tell her that her friend Aecia likes me too."

"That's very funny and very untrue mister."

"Maybe that's how you feel now but I'll make you change you mind later."

"I will my backpack now. That's our house with the green and brick down on the corner. I can walk the rest of the way by myself. I'd let you walk me to the door but if my father is watching, he'll want to meet you and I can tell you are not ready to meet him."

"So what if he is watching? What will you tell him about me?"

"I'll laugh and say, "relax dad; he's just another boring soldier with a crush on that cute little girl that works part time at the library." Then he'll say, "why didn't you invite him in?"

"So you get walked home by a lot of soldiers?"

"No, you're the first one."

"You're a big tease aren't you?"

"No I'm not Rich. Here's my number. You can call me later but don't get the wrong ideal. I just want to continue our conversation."

When I called three hours later, a man with a deep booming voice answered the phone.

"Hello, may I speak to Aecia?"

"Who is this and what do you want with Aecia he snapped?"

"My name is Private First Class Newell."

"Well Private soldier boy.., Aecia is at college. She doesn't have time for a soldier boy! You stay away from her! My daughter is going to make something of her and she can't do that if you soldier boys are always calling her!" Click....

I waited an hour and called back.

Hello said the same voice that I had heard earlier.

"Uh, may I speak to Aecia?"

"Your voice sounds familiar. Didn't I just tell you that she wasn't here?" Son, don't call back or you'll be sorry!"

What's his problem? I thought. Why didn't Aecia tell me that she was in college? The next day I went to the library. Her father had shook me up so badly that I had forgotten to take my books but it didn't matter this trip was to talk to Miss Aecia. I found her in the back sorting through some old books.

"Why didn't you tell me you were in college? I blurted out loud enough for everyone to hear."

"Shhh, keep it down. This is a library mister."

"I called you a couple of times yesterday and I kept getting your father."

"Really...that must have been interesting. Where are your books?"

"I forgot them."

"That's not good Rich, not good at all. I know how important your studies are to you. I guess I'm a bad influence on you."

"Will you just listen for a moment Aecia? Your father did not seem too thrilled about me calling you or those other guys calling either."

"What other guys? What did dear old dad say?"

"He told me not to call you and hung up the phone."

"What did you do then?"

"I waited about an hour and called back."

I could see a smile quickly dash across her face and then it was gone.

"Oh don't worry about him since the divorce he feels like he has to be this knight in shining armor and protect me from the demons."

"What demons?"

"You of course."

"Me?"

"Yeah you know, men."

"But you said demons."

"What's the difference? Anyway, don't worry about him. He's just a big old teddy bear."

"Well...he sounded more like a grizzly bear to me."

"I get off in two hours. If you hang around and I'll let you walk me home."

"I'm not really up to another long walk. We ran ten miles this morning for PT.

"Well…I guess I'll see you later then."

"Alright, I'll walk you home but I'll be next door at the bowling alley until you get off."

As I was walking out of the library the old librarian motioned for me to come over. "Follow me" she whispered. I followed her into her office.

"Have a seat young man. Your name is Rich correct."

"Yes Miss McGowan. What did I do?"

"You seem to be a nice young man. I can tell Aecia is very fond of you. She is like a daughter to me. You will not find anyone as sweet and caring as she. If you mistreat her in any way you will have me to deal with. Do you understand?"

"Yes I do."

"I'll be watching you. You may leave now."

I stood up to leave and notice that my hands were shaking. What kind of soldier was I that I could be so easily scared by a sixty year old lady?

As I set on the bench in the bowling alley with smoke choking me, several things kept running through my head. The most pressing one at the moment was how did I just roll back to back gutter balls? The other was Aecia's posse. If her father didn't get me; I'm sure the old librarian would.

I was awakened from my day dream state by a distant voice that seemed to be calling my name. Aecia was sitting next to me putting on bowling shoes.

"Has it been two hours already?"

"No, it's only been about thirty minutes. I left early. I want you to teach me how to bowl."

"Trust me. I'm really not that good at it."

"I'm a quick learner just teach me what you know. I'll figure out the rest myself."

"The first thing you need to do is develop a stance. Let me see how you are going to stand before you take steps to throw the ball. Open your legs a little wider."

"Oh you would like that wouldn't you Mr. Rich."

"Just concentrate on what you are doing Aecia before you hit someone with that ball!"

I watched her roll her first ball. It went straight down the center but left two pins standing.

"Are you sure you never did this before?"

"I never said I hadn't bowled before. I just wanted you to teach me, "soldier boy".

"Very funny, I see you take after your father."

"Oh no, I'm much more like my mother."

"Where is she?"

"I'm sorry. I don't want to talk about that right now."

"Are you Ok?"

"I'm a little sensitive when it comes to my mom."

"I'm sorry Aecia. I didn't mean to upset you."

"I don't feel like bowling anymore. Can you call me a taxi?

"I thought we were going to walk."

"I don't feel like (sob) walking anymore."

"Are you crying?"

"It's nothing...please call me a taxi."

"Can I ride with you?"

"Yes."

When the taxi got to her house she was very close to tears. She had been laying her head on my shoulder the entire time and hadn't said a word. I didn't know what to do. The change in her had happen so quickly. She went from being this joking cute little bowler to this sad little girl in less than fifteen seconds. It was very apparent that she wasn't ready to talk about it.

I walked her to the door and asked her to let me stay with her until she felt better. She started crying and said softly, "you have to promise to leave before my dad gets home." I promised that I would. When we went inside I was impressed with her home. She showed me the kitchen and the living room.

"Make yourself comfortable Rich."

"What time does your father get home?"

"In three days...

"Did you say in three days?"

"Yes, remember you promised to leave before he gets here. Make yourself comfortable. I'll be back down soon."

It was a Friday afternoon, which meant her father would be gone the entire weekend. What in the world was going on! I found the stereo and turned on the radio. There was a big picture of her and a bunch of kids. I picked it up, sat on the couch and waited for my little friend to join me. When she did I almost fell off the couch. She had taken a shower and was wearing a short housecoat that revealed those beautiful legs but instead of sitting on the couch with me she sat across the room.

"Are you Ok now?"

"Maybe?"

"What does maybe mean?"

"Well you asked if you could stay until I was Ok, so if I say I'm Ok you might leave. I don't want you to leave."

"I can stay as long as you want me to."

"Good, I'm alone so much. It will be nice to spend time with someone.
Be careful with that picture."

"Who are all these kids?"

"I do volunteer work at the center for homeless kids."

"How long have you been doing that?"

"This is my third year. Normally when I take a taxi from the library that's where I'm headed. That's why I was so upset that day when I fell."

"I thought it was me that you were mad at."

"Not exactly, the truth is I sort of staged the whole thing."

"What do you mean?"

"Well, except for falling and bruising my legs the whole thing was staged. I had planned to only drop a few books but you were late that day and the taxi was coming."

"You're right. I was about fifteen minutes late. Are you telling me that you knew exactly what time I'd get there?"

"Most of the time, I can set my watch by you. I didn't realize that all you would care about was looking up my dress and staring at my legs."

"I wasn't looking up your dress but you do have beautiful legs. How is that bruise?"

"Come over here and see for yourself. It's much better but be careful. It's still a little sore."

"I'll be gentle. You have great legs and the bruise is hardly noticeable now. If you wanted to get my attention all you had to do was come say hi. Besides, you already had my attention the moment I saw you. So how long can I stay?"

"How about you stay the entire weekend?"

"Did you say the entire weekend?"

"Please say you will. We can watch movies and play games. It will be fun."

"Ok, but I need to go get some clothes."

"No you don't. I'm afraid if you go, you won't come back."

"I promise I'll be back. I really want to spent time with you."

"Don't worry. I'm sure I can find something for you to wear. Then we really don't have to leave the house."

"You mean stay inside the house the entire weekend."

"Yep, besides, if the neighbors see us coming and going someone might say something to my dad."

"How often do you do things like this?"

"This is the first time."

"Well Ok, I guess."

"Great, you pick out a movie. I'll call and order us a pizza. What do you like on your pizza?"

"It doesn't matter, I'll eat almost anything."

"How about extra cheese, mushrooms and sausage?"

"That will be fine."

"There is some coke and some fruit drinks in the fridge. I think my father has some beer in their also but don't drink it all."

"I don't drink beer."

"Really...I thought all soldiers drank that crap."

"Not me sweetheart."

"Don't call me sweetheart Rich. It only confuses things. Here is a pair of my dad's pajamas. You go take a shower and join me on the love seat afterwards. The pizza should be here by then."

"Ok a shower sounds like a good idea. Will you come wash my back?"

"I don't think that's a good plan Mr. Rich. You have pretty long arms. I think they will reach all the spots."

The love seat was the perfect size. Aecia got a blanket and crawled into my arms and fell asleep after the first thirty minutes. She felt so good in my arms. I got bold and caressed one of her breasts. She immediately woke up and calmly said if you want to keep that hand attached to your arm, you'll make sure that doesn't happen again.

I apologized and she was now wide awake. After we watched two movies and stuffed ourselves with pizza I was sleepy and ready for bed. She kissed me on the cheek and said thanks for staying with me.

"Aecia does this mean we are going to play husband and wife?"

"No it doesn't."

"Does it mean we are going steady?"

"It does not."

"Then what does it mean?"

"Oh, only that I've completely lost my mind?"

"That was my next guess. I only have one last question. Where will I be sleeping?"

"You will be on that couch, right over there mister."

"Are you going to leave me down here by myself?"

"Why are you afraid?"

"No, I just like the thought of sleeping in the same bed as you."

"No way, you've already shown me that you can't keep your hands to yourself but then again I know it must be hard for you to control yourself in the presence of such a beautiful girl."

"I promise to behave. Can I please sleep with you?"

"I'm sorry but that's not going to happen besides, I thought you wanted a pretty girl."

"You are pretty Aecia."

"No, I'm just a plain Jane but you can come up and tell me a bedtime story. Do you promise to behave yourself? Do you promise?"

"Yes I do"

"This is a nice bedroom."

"Thank you."

"I could be very comfortable here. It really beats the heck out of my bed at the barracks."

"What kind of bedtime story are you going to tell me?"

"I have the perfect bedtime story for you. Are you ready?"

"Let me brush my teeth and I'll be right there."

"This is a true story but it's also scary. It's about the time I was in Panama for jungle training."

"What's so scary about that?"

"Listen and you will see."

"We left Fort Campbell in February so it was cold here. I had a very high temperature and was probably close to the flu but when we arrived in Panama it was eighty degrees and I felt great. We were stationed on the beach. It was a very nice area.

At night I would go down to the beach and cover myself in sand. The only thing missing was someone to share it with.

"There were other soldiers there. Couldn't you share it with them?"

"I'm talking about a woman!"

"Ok Rich, ha, ha."

"Any way the wind blew in off the sea and it smelled good. I was starting to like this Army thing. Our first two days in Panama we toured the jungle zoo and were instructed which animals to avoid when we were in the jungle. The things that the instructor keep harping on were snakes, monkeys and poison needles called black palm that grew up to five inches long on the trees deep in the jungle.

"All of these things are dangerous!" he shouted. Don't mess with any of them he repeated over and over again. Now, we could understand about the snakes and we also understood that the black palm needles were poisonous... but what was this monkey business all about?

That little monkey was the same monkey that sits on the shoulders of the guy on the street who plays music with a tin cup collecting money. It couldn't possibly cause us any harm. We were the 101st Air Assault infantry and we weren't afraid of anything or anybody.

The next day we were on our first training mission in the jungle. I thought it was strange how many different sounds the animals made as we traveled through the jungle. Our 1st Sergeant was a veteran of the last two wars and he was watching us from the flank. I guess he wanted to see if we really knew what we were doing.

At noon we finally stopped for lunch. Everyone seemed to be in a joyous mood. For most of us it was our first time in the jungle. All of a sudden there was a lot of laughing and cussing coming from the front of the camp.

Apparently a monkey had relieved himself on one of the guy's heads and everyone was laughing like crazy. Like a madman the soldier starting yelling and threw his steel helmet up into the tree. There was a small shriek and the little monkey fell out of the tree onto the ground.

We were all stunned at this sudden change of events. The soldier was walking around in a circle spitting on the monkey. He took out his penis to urinate on the monkey but the 1st Sergeant burst out of the formation and knocked him to the ground.

"What do you think you're doing?" he yelled! You killed it! Get your sorry butt over in those woods and dig a hole to bury it in. Then dig one next to it, so I can bury your good for nothing ass in!"

The jungle had suddenly grown quiet or maybe it had been quiet for some time now. All we could hear was the 1st Sergeant yelling at Private Barlow.

I've always been told even before joining the military that soldiers are not too bright and what Private Barlow had just done was not only stupid but also heartless. The holes were dug, one for the monkey and one for Private Barlow.

"Did he really put Private Barlow in the Hole?"

"Yes he did Aecia, now listen."

We stood there unable to believe that he was actually putting Barlow in the hole and throwing dirt on top of him.

Our squad leader, Sergeant Wilson was one of the most likable people I had ever met. He was from the Island of Jamaica. He kept shaking his head and reminding us that we had been warned not to mess with the monkeys. We better pray, he repeated over and over again, we better pray.

Thirty minutes later we were walking through the jungle again. I don't know if it was the sadness of seeing the little monkey killed or the doom and gloom of Sergeant Wilson's praying but the sudden quietness of the jungle had me very scared.

The same jungle that had been so alive all morning was now like walking through a crypt. At three o'clock that afternoon we had to cross a river that was almost a quarter of a mile wide. For most of us this was no problem at least not until the 1st Sergeant informed us that we had to pretend that one soldier in each squad was injured and had to be carried across the river on a make shift raft.

This was not an easy task but once we had finally crossed the river we stopped and made camp. Most of us were still in shock over the day's events. Some of us were just plain tired. It's amazing how tiring it can be to carry someone across a river. We had walked ten miles through the jungle and we all needed some rest.

"Rich ten miles is not that far."

"Woman please stop interrupting me. Do you want me to finish the story or not?"

"I'm sorry, go on."

"Anyway ten miles through the jungle is more like twenty or thirty miles.

As I was putting up my tent for the night I got the bad news that I would have guard duty that night. It was only one hour shifts but, it was at the worst time, 3:00 a.m. which meant I didn't get to go back to bed because we woke up at 4:30 a.m.

Just before dusk I finished with my tent and laid down for about 20 minutes. I lay there wondering why I had chosen this crazy life for myself. Just as I drifted off to sleep, I heard a loud scream that sent shivers down my spine and made me sit straight up.

At first I thought I was dreaming until I heard it again. It sounded as if someone had just been pushed over the edge of a cliff. We were aware that the *Contras* were less than fifty miles away. But how did they get pass the barricades? They were the reason, we were doing the "jungle training" in the first place. So we could kick their butts in the event that they started trouble.

I slowly crawled to the edge of my tent and peeped out to get a better look. I quickly ducked back in when I heard several more screams. These came from a different direction than the first. I was shaking like a leaf in a typhoon at this point.

"What was happening Rich? Who were these people?"

"I knew I couldn't just hide in my tent. I was a soldier. This is what I got paid to do. Besides, if I stayed there, they would find me soon any way. So I crawled out of my tent. It was so dark that I couldn't see my hand in front of my face. Suddenly, there was another scream and a machine gun was firing.

I stood up to get a better view of what was going and there was another scream. What I didn't realize is that this scream was coming from me. Something was around my neck!

"Oh my God Rich! What did you do?"

"I was trying to get it off me and screaming dear God, dear God what is going on? Whatever had me would not let go. I quickly realized that the entire camp was under attack. Soldiers were yelling and cussing. We didn't have any real bullets, so we were going to have to fight our way out of this conflict. Suddenly, the sky lit up and what I saw sent shock waves through my nervous system.

"What did you see Rich? Solider boy what did you see?"

"There were hundreds of them Aecia….

"Hundreds of what Rich?"

"Monkeys...

"What...did you say monkeys?"

"Yes as far as the eyes could see Aecia. Monkeys were everywhere and they were kicking our butts."

"You're joking right?"

"No, I'm not joking. We were getting our butts kicked by monkeys."

"Ha ha, Rich stop...you mean to tell me that the brave 101st, "we ain't afraid of nobody," was getting their butts kicked by a bunch of little monkeys? Ha ha, please tell me you are joking."

"I wish I were."

"This is so funny. I thought this was supposed to be a scary story."

"It is a scary story but maybe...you had to be there."

"Rich that is the funniest story I've ever heard. I can't wait to tell this story to my friends."

"No! You can never tell anyone. Promise me!"

"You're starting to scare me a little Rich."

"Just promise me that you'll never repeat this story to any one!"

"You seem so serious Rich."

"I guess you had to be there Aecia."

"So what did the brave 101st do next?"

"We did the only thing that we could do. We built campfires and spent the entire night awake."

"Ha, ha, were you the Army or the boy scouts?"

"That's very funny Aecia, very funny."

"Were you afraid they might come back?"

"Yes, that's exactly what we were afraid of."

"I'm sorry Rich but I don't believe this story. It's funny. I just don't believe it."

"Good…I think it's better that you don't believe it. But do you know why I was so scared?"

"Please tell me why?"

"I never told anyone but when I was putting up my tent I killed a snake."

"Oh Rich…ha, ha, ha. You my friend are quite the story teller. I can't wait to hear what you'll tell me tomorrow night."

"Very funny Aecia…I'm going to bed."

"Goodnight Rich…ha, ha, ha.

She kept her word and made me sleep on the couch the entire weekend. My back ached for weeks but my heart was alive.

"That's a cute story Rich."

"Resa...I thought I asked you not to interrupt me."

"I'm sorry. I thought the story was over."

"No there is more."

"I'm sorry "soldier boy" ha, ha, please continue."

"Well...I continued to chase her and three months later she softly whispered in my ear, "wake up sleepy head, it's time to get up." Slowly, I force my eyes open. She smelled so good and had on nothing but a bath towel wrapped loosely around her body.

My instinct was the same as any man's who wakes up and finds a beautiful lady standing beside his bed, but like always she managed to stay just out of reach.

I didn't have to look at the clock to know it was still early. I roll over and try to get a little more sleep.

"Rich it's such a beautiful morning. Let's go for a walk."

"Sweetheart, are you forgetting that I worked last night?"

She climbed in bed and starts to gently massage my back and nibbled on my ear and neck. Suddenly, I'm wide-awake. Her young body's intense heat feels like a volcano that's about to erupt for the first time. She climbs on top of me and looks me dead in the eyes and utters that dreaded word...please. Oh, how I hated it when she did that! I know it won't do me any good to argue at this point. It never does. I get up and find my snickers.

She starts humming her favorite tune, which normally means she has gotten her way.

"What has you in such a good mood this morning, I ask."

She smiles and says, "you do my love." She continued to hum without missing a beat.

She sits in my favorite chair and puts on her worn out running shoes. Why she doesn't wear her good shoes is beyond me. There they sat my two most favorite things in the whole world. My woman and my chair. A chair that was lucky to still be in this house.

Two weeks earlier I came home for lunch and found it sitting on the curb with the rest of the trash. Aecia had once made the comment that I loved that chair more than her. A comment that I thought was just completely ludicrous.

I had found that chair at a garage sale in the rich part of town. It was almost brand new and for only five dollars I had to have it. I remember thinking that the color left a lot to be desired but it was so comfortable and would be perfect for watching the game.

I had been in the Army a year and a half and I wasn't making very much money, so I was always looking for a deal. That chair was a steal.

As we walked though the park my mind starts to drift.

"What are you thinking about Rich?"

"Just how proud I am of you. In a couple of months you will be graduating from college. I was just wondering what you are going to do?"

"Well, there are so many things to consider and I'm not completely sure about what I'll be doing but the most important thing is that it's somewhere close to you."

"That sounds nice Aecia, but let's be honest with ourselves. You will probably receive job offers for all over the world and let's not forget that I'm in the Army and I will be heading oversees in about a year."

"Rich, my love…you are going to be the father of my six kids someday. I promise to always love you and where ever you are is where I want to be."

She sealed her statement with a kiss.

"Is there anything else on your mind Rich?"

"Did I hear you say six kids? Yesterday you said four kids."

"Well I changed my mind. I can do that can't I?"

"You can do anything you want pretty lady."

"Now, is there anything else on your mind?"

"Well, as a matter of fact there is this one little thing." *I stood there looking at her in her tight little jogging suit.* "I wish you didn't wear you clothes so tight."

"What do you mean?"

"Well you have such a shapely body and everything you wear seems to show every curve. It's very uncomfortable when we are out in public and I see how people stare at you. The men and the women stare. Not to mention how it affects me physically."

"Oh Rich, please, not that again! If I've told you once I've told you a thousand times. I'm not having sex until I'm married. We've talked about this and I thought you understood how I feel."

She stopped and sat on a bench and said, "I will go shopping tonight and buy a few new outfits. If you are good, I'll model them for you tonight. Anything that you don't like I'll take back." She leaned over to kiss me but instead whispers, "last one back to the apartment has to do the dishes for a week." Then like a rocket she took off."

I would like to say I won the race but the truth of the matter was I liked the view of her from behind as well as from the front. One thing that the Army had taught me is there are a time to lead and a time to follow. This indeed was a time to follow!

We took a shower together and had break-fast that consisted of pancakes, strawberries and kiwi. I did the dishes and went to the den to con-tinue working on my novel. At that point in my life, I had dreams of someday being rich and I thought being an author and an artist would help me achieve that dream.

When I write hours seem like seconds. Some days the words come so easy, I can write for days and only take a break to go to the bathroom but there are days when all I can do is sit there and stare at a blank sheet of paper and wonder why the words won't come.

Today I wasn't having any problem writing. Aecia pop in once and said something but I'm not sure what it was. She was aware by now that when I write there could be an earthquake and I wouldn't notice.

Suddenly, there was a sweet aroma in the air. I turn around to find Aecia standing there with her hands on her hips. I looked at the clock and quickly noticed that almost four hours had passed since I starting writing. Where did the time go?

"I guess you didn't hear me blowing the horn Mr. Spielberg. I can't wait until you are finished with that book. Is there anything in there about me yet?"

"No, I said slowly shaking my head as I looked into her eyes. I'm afraid not sweetheart.

I can't let the world know that someone as wonderful as you exists. I think it's best that I keep you a secret for as long as possible."

I could feel her melt as I stared at her from top to bottom. I slowly paused at her waist and again at her breasts. When my eyes met hers, I saw something in them that I hadn't seen before.

She took my hand and said, "come help me. I've got some things down stairs in the car."

She said she was going shopping and judging from the amount of bags, she had done just that. She even bought a small gift for me but said I couldn't open it until later tonight.

After we unloaded the car she took my arms and wrapped them around her luscious body and gave me an incredibly sensuous kiss. I could feel the nipples on her breasts harden and she could feel the same from my penis. She whispered go back to your novel my love but I said no. I want this moment to last forever. She kissed me again and sent me back to my novel and she went into the bedroom.

At 5:00 p.m. Aecia entered the room wearing one of her new outfits.

"Lets go out tonight Rich. It will be my treat. You can pick the restaurant."

I sat there unable to move or utter a simple word. I could not take my eyes off her. She looked absolutely magnificent.

She was wearing a blue evening gown with an off white stole draped over her shoulder. She slowly turned so that I could see her completely. When her eyes met mine they seemed to ask, "do you like this outfit, Big Daddy?" My eyes told her yes, "yes I do!" I started to get up and walk toward her but she softly said, "don't move the show has just begun, and I need you to sit right there, until I'm done."

She gracefully made her exit. A few moments later she entered the room again but before she did she told me to close my eyes and not to open them until she said so. I could feel her presence as she got closer. The perfume she was wearing was out of this world. It smelled like a combination of rose petals, honey suckle and a smell that was unmistakably Aecia!

When she finally asked me to open my eyes, she was standing next to the window wearing a purple teddy with a green lace. The light coming though the window allowed me to see her sensational body underneath the teddy, a trick that I'm sure she was aware of.

When she moved, she seemed to float across the room. As she moved closer to me the floating became a slow hypnotic dance. After she teased me to the point of no return she slowly, gracefully retreated into the bedroom. Once again I was ordered not to move and to keep my eyes closed.

This time I could feel her as she walked straight toward me. She stopped just inches directly in front of me. She took my hand and placed it on her face. I started to touch every inch of her face and like a blind man with a good memory who had long ago lost his sight, I could see and feel the love and beauty of what I was touching.

I was almost nineteen and sex was not new to me. Aecia was twenty and claimed to be a virgin. I wanted to believe her but I couldn't get pass the fact that a virgin could be such a tease.

How did she learn to tease like this? How much more of this was I suppose to take?

"Run your fingers through my hair Rich."

She had long hair that she liked to wear in a ponytail. I liked her to wear it down. It drove me crazy the way it laid across her breasts when she combed it at bedtime. If she only knew how many times I woke up in the middle of the night because of a dream I had just had of her.

"You can open your eyes now."

I slowly opened my eyes. I think what will she be wearing? This time I was a little surprised but not disappointed.

She was wearing one of my old tee shirts. It was one that she was very fond of and wore to bed often. I really liked the way her nipples showed through the shirt. She smiled and once again slowly turned so that I could get a complete look at her. After she knew I had got an eyeful, she came and sat on my lap.

I thought I was going to explode. I was sure I would lose it. Aecia kissed me softly on the forehead and nibbled on my ear while whispering. I've tried not to be sexy Big Daddy but no matter what I wear the way you look at me makes me feel sexy. It doesn't matter if I wear an evening gown, a teddy or one of your old tee shirts, you look at me the very same way every time and it makes me feel so sexy.

All I could do was smile. Once again she had made her point. She got up and went to the bedroom and suddenly there was soft music playing.

"Come open your present Rich."

I thought I detected a slight tremble in her voice. I had almost forgotten about that present. It was in such a small box and it was so light. What in the world could it be?

I slowly opened my present as Aecia sat on the edge of the bed staring at me but not saying a word. There was only a small-engraved note inside the small box. I read it slowly.

Rich, you are the love of my life and someday soon I hope to be your wife. Our time together has been great and tonight I'm ready to tempt fate. In my eyes you are my husband already therefore this gift I give to you because I'm ready.

I read the note again not completely sure what it meant until I looked at Aecia and noticed a single tear rolling down her cheek. She then smiled, laid down on the bed and said, "sweetheart please come here, I'm ready…"

The next two months we took our relationship to a new level. Aecia planned the wedding for May 17th. That gave us less than two months to prepare. Her father didn't approve. Her mom who was finally out the institution was happy but reserved. She said she wasn't ready to be a grandmother. They thought we were too young.

"What's the rush?" her father keeps saying. Once he pulled me to the side and promised to have me killed "execution style" if his daughter was pregnant.

I believed that they didn't want to see their successful daughter married to a GI. The only reason they gave in was above all they could see how happy Aecia was.

Our wedding was to take place three days after her graduation in the meantime she had to prepare for finals, so there was no time for me. I decided to go home and visit my family. When I arrived home I was so tired. My cousin Ralph and my brother, Darryl, greeted me in the front yard of my parent's home. Darryl said they were going fishing and wanted me to come but I was too tired. We talked for a few minutes and they left. I went and took a nap. Two hours later I woke up to a loud noises coming from outside. There were kids in the yard yelling and crying. All I could understand was that Darryl was in the pond where they had been fishing.

At first I didn't realize what this meant until they said he had fallen out of the boat. There wasn't a car, so I took off running to the pond, which was two miles away. I got there before anyone else. I was alone and the pond seemed so big, I guess I expected to see him sitting on the bank or something...but he wasn't.

All I could see was the pond. It never looked so large before. A few minutes after I got there a group of people showed up with my mother. They wouldn't let me go in the water to search for his body. In my mind I kept expecting to see him jump up out of the pond and run to me and say he was Ok. Instead the men that had gone into the pond found him and carried his lifeless body out.

I was numb. It felt like the sky had just opened up. I couldn't cry at the moment. Our mom was crying enough for us all. I just could not believe what was happening. Just two hours ago he was standing beside me talking, laughing and smiling that little smile of his. If only I had gone with them, if only I had gone with them, I thought. They tried CPR but it did no good...my brother was gone.

He was only eighteen, his life was just beginning. Everyone loved him. No one had ever said a bad thing about him. Vonda and her brother were the first one's to come see about me. They had lost their older brother while we were still in high school. As I lay in my bed crying, my friend Marcus told me that time is the only thing that can make you feel better. I know you don't believe me right now but you'll see, he said.

"It's going to be Ok Rich." He repeated this several times.

I still hadn't called Aecia and told her. I could not bring myself to speak the words. It was actually the next day before I called her.

When I finally told her, she insisted that she was coming but I asked her not to. She had finals the next couple of weeks and that's what I wanted her to concentrate on. She called me several times a day everyday. I needed her with me but I couldn't be selfish. We both knew she needed to concentrate on her tests.

"When are you coming back?" she asked.

I told her that I was in a lot of pain and my family needed me but I would be back soon. She asked if I wanted to postpone the wedding...a wedding that I hadn't told my parents about yet. Part of the reason that I had come home was to give them the good news about Aecia. A wonderful girl that they had heard about but didn't realize was about to become their daughter-in-law, in less than three weeks.

She understood that I had been through a lot. She kept saying that all she wanted to do was hold me in her arms and make the pain go away. I wanted and needed her with me so badly. She was five hundred miles away, "it might as well have been five million miles."

"I miss you so much and mom and dad ask about you everyday."

"Tell them I said hi and that I'll be Ok as long as I have you in my life."

She told me that she loved me and hung up the phone.

A week after the funeral my Army Commander called and told me I had to come back to Fort Campbell, Kentucky. They had already given me a four day extension. I wasn't ready but I knew I had to go back.

When I called Aecia and told her that I'd be there in two days she was so happy. It had been almost two weeks since I'd seen her and I couldn't wait. I'll make you a special dinner she said and we can snuggle and you know….

I took the Greyhound back to Ft. Campbell, a fourteen-hour ride. It was a terrible trip. Unfortunately, you couldn't fly there from my home town. If so Aecia would have been able to come see me. I tried to call her several times on my miserable journey but I couldn't reach her. I tried to sleep on the bus but all I could think about was seeing her pretty face and holding her in my arms.

When the bus finally arrived, it was almost midnight. I made a vow to never ever ride the bus again. It was time I invested in a car. I had the taxi take me straight to Aecia's parent's house. She had been staying with them since I had been away. I knocked on the door but no one answered and strangely there were no cars in the yard. I waited on the porch for about two hours. Finally a car pulled up in the driveway. A gentleman that I had never seen before got out.

"Hello young man, you must be Rich."

"Yes I am."

"Let's go in the house for a minute."

"Who are you?"

"I'm Aecia's uncle. My name is Marshall. I've heard a lot about you. I was sorry to hear about your brother."

"Thank you, it was very tough. Where's Aecia?"

"I think you should sit down Rich."

"Sit down for what?"

"Its Aecia."

"What about her?"

"There was an accident this morning. I'm sorry son but she's in pretty bad shape."

"What happened? Where is she?"

"Calm down. I know this is a shock but try to calm down and listen to what I'm saying. This morning she was going to the store and a semi was trying to merge into her lane but there just wasn't enough room. It hit the side of her car and it flipped several times. She's in General hospital right now. Her mother told me that you were coming in tonight and they knew you'd come straight here."

As I sat there trying to understand why this stranger was lying to me, my mind and body seem to have separated. I wanted to yell liar, liar and wake up from this horrible nightmare.

He was still talking and I had no idea what he was saying until he came over and practically lifted me off the couch. I leaned on him as he carried me to the car. I was crying so hard

I couldn't see. I didn't think I had any tears left after my brother died.

Everything went dark. I don't remember the drive to the hospital, I only remember him helping me out of the car. When we got to the room I could see her parents kneeling beside her bed. There were a lot of people in the hallway and I could feel their eyes on me.

When I went inside her room I looked down at the bed and almost fainted. Dear God, who is this? What a terrible trick to play on someone. This is not her, I said softly. Her father took my hand and said hello Rich; she's been waiting for you.

They moved away from the bed so that I could get closer. I looked into her eyes and for the first time I saw Aecia. I knew I had to be strong for her so I took her hand and I felt a very slight squeeze. I leaned over and kissed her on the cheek. She smiled I think...then closed her eyes and my world fell apart.

They had to pull me from the room. I kept thinking please let this be a dream but it wasn't.

I hurt too bad and I knew the hurt was real or I would have woke up long ago. That was twenty years ago and I still wake up some nights with my pillow wet from the tears I cry in my sleep.

Resa, I try not to think about a marriage that was only a week away and the kids that she always talked about. Just how long it takes to recover from the loss of a loved one can never be measured in time. I believe as long as the mind is able to remember the heart will never completely heal. I'm still close with her family to this day.

They have told me a thousand times that she would want me to get on with my life. I say to them, "she was my life. So you see Resa; Karen is not the one that I long for. That's the end of my story except for one thing. Before I went to visit my family Aecia told me that she thought she was pregnant."

"I'm so sorry Rich (sob) that is such a sad story. It's starting to rain. I think everyone in heaven just heard that story and now they are also crying. I think I'll go take a nap."

Resa…

"Yes Rich."

"Thank you for listening. It meant a lot to me. You are the only person that I have told this story."

"You're welcome Rich and you did say it's been twenty years didn't you?"

"Yes it has Resa but it's been a short twenty years. Maybe, I'll write a story about her some-day. Maybe, then the healing can began?"

"I think the healing began when you told me this story. You need to love again Rich. I think she would want that for you. You need to really think about that."

"Love is not an easy thing to find Resa. That's one of the reasons it hurts so bad when you lose it."

"I've never been in love Rich and I'm not sure I ever want to be. Goodnight my friend. I'll talk to you later."

"Goodnight Resa."

Chapter 8

It took Malloy over an hour to find the old case and it took him another hour to read through the sloppy mess. The papers were so old that it was difficult to read. It also looked like someone had gone through the file recently and didn't care to put it back in order.

There was no information about the daughter. She was only ten years old at the time of her mother's death so there should have been mention of custody by a family relative or adoption. The total file was seventeen pages but two of them were missing. What was on page four and eleven? Why were these pages missing and who took them?" wondered Malloy.

This was a dead end.

"Well it's about time that you came from down there," said Henry. I was about to send someone to look for you. Did you at least find what you were looking for?"

"No I didn't." Something is not right about that case. The girl didn't just disappear but someone is trying to make it look as though she did. My question is why?"

"Why are you worrying your fool self over a case that's over thirty years old Malloy? Aren't you approaching retirement soon?"

"Yes I am Henry but what does that have to do with anything."

"I just think you ought to be relaxing more. Let the young bucks handle this."

"When this case first hit, "we were the young bucks Henry." Tell me this…to your knowledge has anyone been going through those files lately?"

"I can't say exactly but you are welcome to check the log and see who's been going down there."

"Can I make a copy of the log and take with me."

"Nope…not allowed and you know I can't do that but you can look over the log and write down any names that you want."

"Damn Henry, you are not making this easy for me."

"Malloy, you are lucky that I'm letting you look at the books. Relax there has only been seven entries in the past two years. Not a lot of people wanting to poke around in the basement at those old files. Here take a look. You should be able to remember a couple of names."

"There is only one name that rings a bell," said Malloy. Warren Gray…when was that asshole here?

"It's right there in the ledger Sergeant. He signed in two days ago at 9:00am and signed out at 10:15am."

"That explains why the file was in such a mess."

"Do you think he was looking at the same file that you were?"

"Of course I do. He also took the two missing pages."

"What missing papers and how can you be sure it was him?"

"It was him. I'm sure of it. What I'm not sure about is why. Thanks for your help Henry. I'll talk to you later."

"Just one more thing before you leave."

"What is it?"

"Well Malloy, I'm not one to believe everything I hear or to spread a lot of gossip but it appears to me that you might be getting your fool self involved in something that might be better left alone. Now this girl has been missing for over forty years and now you are getting all bent out of shape over the whole thing like it happened yesterday. I know you have a mind of your own and nothing that I'm going to say is going to change that but I believe if you don't let this one rest we are going to be attending your funeral in the not too distant future."

"Thanks for the words of wisdom and the words of concern Henry but neither is necessary. I'm not content to just ride off into retirement as a patrol cop. I need more than that."

"What you need is to find yourself a woman. What about that old girl that you used to hang out with at the bowling alley?"

"She started hanging out with someone else. Now if you have no more questions, I really must be on my way."

"You're not fooling me Malloy. I know this is about your old man. He couldn't solve this case and neither will you."

"This has nothing to do with me Pops!"

"Sure it does, I can't say that I blame you. If someone had done those things to my dad, I would react the same way that you are. However, I don't think it would have taken me thirty years to do so."

"This discussion is over Henry!"

"Ok, Malloy but the sooner you face the truth the better off you'll be. There is nothing but trouble headed your way my friend. Leave that gas station and those who run it alone! You do it Malloy or prepare to meet your maker…"

"What is Henry talking about?" thought Malloy. He just had to bring me Pops into this didn't he? Well this is not about my dad. The police said that his car blew up because of a faulty gas line but I'm not buying it." Something or someone didn't want him investigating those murders at that damn gas station. If it kills me I'm going to find out what really happened! There are no such things as ghosts…

Chapter 9

Detective Gray lit a cigarette as he stood next to the traffic light waiting for an opportunity to cross the street. He had a lead and was about to knock on the unsuspecting person's door. It was the only true lead that he had in this case so far and he knew that he had to be careful how he approached this lady. Finally, the light changed and he quickly crossed the street and headed for apartment number 17 on Steeplechase Drive. Once he got there he knocked rather hard on the door and in a few seconds, the door slowly opened.

"Hello Mrs. French. My name is detective Gray. I was wondering if I might ask you a few questions."

"What is this in reference to detective?"

"I'm investigating a murder that took place about two blocks from here three weeks ago. A fellow was on his way to work and someone robbed and killed the old guy."

"I'm sorry detective but I mind my own business and don't know anything about which you are talking about."

"I understand Mrs. French but could you do me one small favor."

"Depends on what the favor is detective. I'm a married woman and should not be doing favors for strange men that suddenly show up at my door."

"Ha, ha, I can agree with that Mrs. French. Yes, I can completely understand your point. The favor that I need is pretty simple Mrs. French. About thirty-years ago you worked at a nursery near 20th and Clover. Isn't that correct?"

"Yes, I did but it was closer to forty-years."

"Really has it been that long? My oh my, how times flies. Anyway, I was hoping that you could look a picture for me. It's an old photo but the faces are in pretty good shape."

"Where's the photo? Please be quick about it. I'm trying to get my husband's dinner ready before he gets home. He doesn't like to wait for his dinner."

"Oh I can understand that. My wife used to do the same for me. God rest her soul."

"Oh your wife died?"

"Yes she did. She had lung cancer. Too many cigarettes, I'm afraid."

"That's a shame detective. My husband smokes also. I've been trying to get him to stop for over twenty years but he is so stubborn. He won't listen to anyone, "that man.""

"Oh my wife never smoked a day in her life. It was second hand smoke that did her in. She fell ill one day and never recovered. There hasn't been a day gone by since she passed two years ago that I haven't wanted to kill myself for subjecting her to my terrible smoking habits."

"I'm truly sorry for your lost Detective. Please show me the picture so I can get back to my wifely duties."

"Here it is. Do you remember these people?"

"Why of course I do. That is the Sanford family. Their daughter use to come to the nursery all the time. The family ran a gas station that was just a few blocks away. It's a shame what happened to her parents."

"What happened to her parents?"

"That was a big story back then. What kind of detective are you that you don't know about that? The gas attendant killed her mother and her German lover. Less than a year after that the father remarried and sold the station to his twin brother. The marriage didn't last though. Some people say that old man Sanford never got over the death of his cheating wife and completely lost his mind. However, other people think that his new wife was only after his money and had him committed to an Asylum. I don't know much about that family after that."

"I'm sorry Mrs. French but I haven't heard about these murders. Where did the murders take place and who is the gas attendant?"

"I'm not surprised that you haven't heard about it detective. There were a lot of things that happened at that spooky place that wasn't reported back then."

"Do you mean at the gas station?"

"Yes that's where I mean but more precisely the garage at the gas station. Now the police said they died of carbon monoxide poisoning because they had the car running while they were making love. Apparently, they fell asleep shortly there after but anyone who knew anything about that place back in those days knew it wasn't carbon monoxide that killed them. It was the spirit of the gas attendant that killed them. Poor Mr. Sanford loved that car but I don't have to tell you about men and their cars. It was a sad thing him finding his wife and her lover like that and on Christmas Eve of all days. I never saw him drive that beautiful car again after that."

"Do you remember what kind of car was it?"

"Sure I do, it was a 57 Chevy. Rumor was he parked it in the garage at his home in West Hempstead and never drove it again. If I was him I would have sold it and been done with it but like I said, "he loved that car."

"Mrs. French are you sure Mr. Sanford had a twin brother?"

"Of course he did."

"What can you tell me about him?"

"Well the little girl, I think her name was Elizabeth, talked about her Uncle all the time. I think his name was Fredrick or Harry. I'm not really sure. Sometimes, I believed she loved him more than her own father. The first time her uncle picked her up from the nursery I thought he was her father. That's how much they looked like each other. Later, I could always tell which one was picking her up simply by the way the little girl reacted when he came through the door.

If her daddy came she would just take his hand and leave but if her uncle came she would run and jump into his arms and he would carry her out on his shoulders. One day he came by and picked her up and I never saw Elizabeth again. "I was sad about that for a long time."

"Thank you so much Mrs. French. It has been a pleasure speaking with you this afternoon. You have been a great help."

"Detective, I have a question for you." When you first knocked on my door you said that you wanted information about the killing that took place two blocks from here. Now, I'm not the smartest apple on the tree but it seems to me that you are more interested in that little girl than you are about solving a murder. I'm finding it hard to believe that one has anything to do with the other."

"That's where you are wrong." I'm afraid that the two have more in common that you might think. Right now, I'm confused about a couple of things but the information that you have just given me really helps my investigation and I thank you very much. Here's my card. If you can think of anything else please feel free to call me and just so that you know, the old man that was killed two blocks from here worked as a gas attendant at the gas station on 19th and Clover."

"You're not talking about old Arnold are you?"

"I'm afraid that I am." Did you know him?"

"Yes I did but that was a long time ago."

"Did you know him well?"

"I'm afraid that I have to go detective. I have your card. If I can think of anything else I will call you. Good bye."

"Have a good day Mrs. French."

Is it my imagination or did she just tell me that she was sleeping with Arnold…this is getting more interesting everyday. I have to follow up on this tid bit of information later…

Mrs. French wiped a tear from her eye as she briefly allowed herself to think back to a cold November day 28 years ago when a man three inches shorter than herself made love to her on the floor of the day care center…it only happened that once but it was enough to last a life time. "Rest in peace Arnold, I will take our secret to my grave."

"So Mr. Sanford had a twin brother. This is an interesting piece of information. Why is this news? Shouldn't the fact that he had a twin brother be common knowledge? Something is wrong with this picture...something is very, very wrong. I'm going to need someone to help me figure out this puzzle and I think I know just the person. Stephanie Clinton, "it's time to call in an old favor."

"Stephanie this is Warren Gray."

"Hello Warren, it's been a while since I've heard from you. What do you need this time?"

"Stephanie, I'm working on a case, a very important case as a matter of fact and I was hoping I could get you to do me a small favor."

"Crazy man no...forget it Gray. I'm not getting involved with you again. I almost lost my job the last time I did you a so called, "small favor." By the way didn't they kick your sorry butt off the force?"

"No sweetheart, they just suggested that I find another line of work."

"Well…what are you calling me for then?"

"It's complicated but I'm working an old case that was never solved and I think I'm on to something."

"So what are you now some kind of private eye?"

"You really know how to hurt a man when he's down lady."

"That's sounds like your wife's job Warren."

"I don't have a wife any more Stephanie."

"You mean she finally got wise enough to leave your sorry ass."

"She died Stephanie."

"Oh, I'm sorry Gray. This is a little bit of a shock. What happened to her?"

"She passed a couple of years ago Stephanie but I really don't feel like talking about it."

"Warren, I've talked to you at least a half dozen times in the past year and you never mentioned a thing about it."

"I didn't see a need to mention it to you. However, there were some lonely nights when I thought about calling you and telling you. I thought maybe I could get you to give me some sympathy sex but I decided against it."

"That's a terrible thing to say Warren!" You were a terrible husband anyway. She could have done a lot better."

"I don't disagree with you on that but I thought you'd be happy to hear that I was back on the market Stephanie."

"Don't kid yourself mister. What we had was just a silly high school fling and that was over twenty-five years ago. I'll never give you the time of day again. I'm afraid that you just don't know how to satisfy me. You never did."

"Are you still seeing that Captain from the 9th precinct?"

"Yes, as a matter of fact I am. We've been together almost seven years now and he satisfies me like no man could."

"That's surprising, considering he's old enough to be your father. What are you going to do in a couple of years when he can't get it up anymore?"

"Honey, I've never been with a man that couldn't get it up, except for you and you were young back then."

"Wait a minute now Stephanie. What about that night at "Look Out Mountain" in the back seat of your father's car? I did get it up that night. Several times, if my memory serves me correct."

"Ok, I admit you were in rare form that night but when you got it up, there still wasn't much there to get excited about. As far as other men, one look at me and their manhood is completely aroused. The Captain might be older than I am but he is still taking care of business. Right now he's giving me all I can handle, "which is more than I could ever say about you." As a matter of fact, I think I'll give him a call now and see if he wants to come over and feast on my body tonight. I've got this sexy little night gown that I bought this weekend just for him. I think he'll like it. Now if you don't mind Warren, this conversation, like most conversations that I have with you is starting to bore me. I have work to do."

"Wait Stephanie…just please do me this one favor and I promise never to bother you again. Please for old times sake. Remember there was a time when you didn't hate my guts."

"Goodbye Warren."

"Come on Stephanie. If I'm right about this, I will be able to get my life back and please don't make me bring up the favor I did your family when your brother robbed that jewelry store a couple of years ago."

"I should kill you Warren…always bringing up the past. What is it you need?"

"Thanks Stephanie, I'm about to fax you three names. I need you to locate the addresses of these people. If my hunch is correct all three of these people are dead and have been for a very long time."

"This is crazy Warren...I can't believe I'm even thinking about helping you. Why do you think these people are deceased, furthermore why don't you just let the dead rest in peace?"

"Trust me Stephanie, if my hunch is correct these poor people haven't been able to rest for the last forty years. Now are you standing next to the fax machine?"

"Yes I am."

"I'm sending the fax now. Once you get it read the names to me."

"Ok the fax is coming through now."

"Read the names to me Stephanie."

"Elizabeth Sanford, Harry Sanford and Arnold Muse. Who are these people?"

"I think they are ghosts."

"What did you say?"

I said, "I think they are ghost."

"You have really lost your freaking mind haven't you Warren Gray?"

"I know it sounds crazy Stephanie but I think I'm right and God help us if I am. How long do you think it will take you to get me the information that I need?"

"Well it's late. Give me two days but I'm not promising anything."

"Stephanie please don't mention this to anyone."

"Don't worry Warren, I don't really want it to get out that I'm looking for ghosts. My lips are sealed."

Chapter 10

"Good morning young lady can you filler up and check the air in my tires."

"Sure thing Sir."

"This old station is starting to look a little better these days. I normally would drive right past here but I see the old garage is open again. Has old man Sanford lost his freaking mind?"

"Why do you say that?"

"How long have you worked here girl!"

"Almost four weeks now."

"Well don't you know about this place and that garage? The old man killed his wife and her lover in the room over the garage and then put them in the car to make it look like an accident. A year before that someone died in that garage. The whole neighborhood thought the placed was haunted and wanted to burn it to the ground but the gas attendant wouldn't let them."

"I never heard about any of that. Are you sure you're not making this up."

"Young lady, I'm sixty years old and have no reason to lie about anything. I am not a liar but you don't have to take my word. Ask old Arnold."

"I'm afraid I can't do that right now. Arnold was robbed and killed over four weeks ago."

"He was? That's a shame but it doesn't surprise me. Anyone that spends much time around this place eventually dies a strange death. There ain't no way they could get me inside that strange building."

"Sir please…you are starting to scare me."

"I'm sorry young lady but as long as the gas attendant stays away, "I don't guess you have any thing to worry about."

"The gas attendant..? Why Sir, "I'm the gas attendant."

"My dear girl, everyone knows that the gas attendant died in that garage three nights before the people in this neighborhood tried to burn this place to the ground or was it three days after the bodies were found in the car...I don't really remember, it's been a long time. My memory is not what it use to be."

"How can that be? You just said that the gas attendant is the one that stopped them from burning the place down."

"I know what I said but it's apparent that you are not listening. The gas attendant would not let them burn this place down because it's his resting ground. For the life of me I can't believe old man Sanford would disturb his resting ground by opening up that freaking garage."

"Are you saying that someone is buried in that garage?"

"Yes, I can't prove it, no one in this neighborhood can but we all know it to be true. At least the ones of us who are still alive and re-member what happened here. Young lady you really don't know about any of this do you? I'm sorry, "I never would have bought it up if I had known that you didn't know." I'll say one thing, "you are probably the only one on this entire island that doesn't."

"The air is fine in your tires and you owe me twelve dollars for the gas. I would greatly ap-preciate it, if you didn't come by here any more but if you feel that you must, please keep your mouth shut." There are no such things as ghost and there is nothing that you can say to make me believe otherwise. Now have a great day!"

"I don't think I'll be stopping here anymore, thank you kindly. I will say this though, I'm not the one that's going to make you believe. You mark my word on that! Goodbye and good luck. Please wash your fingernails. A woman's hands should not look like yours."

"Rich, I just had the strangest conversation with another old man. He pretty much con-firmed what that other old man said. Do you re-member the one that came by here three weeks ago talking about how this place was haunted? Now this old man starts talking about people were killed in that room over the garage and someone called the gas attendant being buried in the garage. He says that we are crazy for opening up the garage again. Is any of the things that these old men are saying true?"

"Well…now Resa don't go getting yourself all worked up about some old man's crazy stories. What I can tell you is that it is true about Arnold killing his wife and her lover in that room but as far as all this talk about the gas attendant that's just an old rumor that became a legend."

"So you knew about this crap and didn't tell me. Wait you said Arnold killed his wife and her lover…but the old man just said that it was Mr. Sanford that killed his wife and her lover. None of this makes any sense to me. Who killed whom and for the love of Christ, will someone please tell me who is the Gas Attendant?"

"Resa sometimes Arnold would make jokes about the gas attendant watching over the place. I didn't really understand what he meant. Arnold could be pretty weird sometimes and he would say crazy stuff when he had a little too much to drink. Arnold led a sad life. I remember him telling me about how he use to live at the airport. He would use the bathroom there, eat there and sleep in his van in the parking lot until it was time to come to work. He felt safe there and he could afford the parking fee. He said that he did that for four months until he could afford to move into an apartment. It happened just in the nick of time to because his old van was about to put him down and winter was just around the corner."

"I don't give a freaking rat's butt about all that Rich. What about the rumor that someone is buried here in this garage?"

"Now I haven't heard about that. It's probably just an old story that someone made up. Besides, I think the police would have investigated something like that? Now stop worrying so much about the ramblings of these old men. In the two years that I've been here nothing strange has ever happened."

"I believe them Rich. I also believe you believe them.

"Resa...you are wrong."

"No I'm not Rich, "not about this." I'm going to find out the truth."

"Well how do you intend to prove your theory?"

"I'm going to dig up the garage and you are going to help me."

"No you're not! Now I've heard about as much of this as I care to."

"Just try to stop me Rich. Those old men aren't lying. I could see the fear and disbelief in this last man's eyes as he stared at this garage. He told me that the people in this neighbor tried to burn this place down but the gas attendant wouldn't let them."

"What's so strange about that Resa?"

"Rich the gas attendant died in this garage three days before they tried to burn this place down."

"For the last freaking time, who is the gas attendant?"

"That's what I want to know Rich, "I have a feeling that he is the last mechanic that old man Sanford hired to work the garage." Now it starting to make sense why the garage was locked and the room upstairs was locked." Rich either Arnold or Mr. Sanford thought they were locking the past away behind those locks on the doors."

"Resa, if these things are indeed true what would make them stay here?"

"I don't know Rich. Maybe they were more afraid of losing their job than they were of any ghosts. Besides, I'm not sure you can run from a ghost. I still think we should dig up the garage."

"We are doing Ok here, leave it alone besides, the ground is as hard as a rock. We would need a bulldozer just to get started."

"Ok Rich, I'll leave it alone for now but I'm not sleeping in that spooky room anymore."

"Good, I'll take the room and you can have the sofa, I hope you have a strong back."

"I'm not sleeping on that old sofa."

"Where you going to sleep then?

"I don't know...maybe the airport."

Chapter 11

"Good morning Malloy. You look like you slept in that suit."

"Good morning Karen. I was up all night thinking about that stupid old case that I mentioned to you last week. I believe that Warren Gray is also investigating the same case."

"Warren Gray you say, now there's a name that you don't hear everyday." There was a time when he was thought to be one of the best detectives here in New York," said Karen.

"Yeah I know. Too bad about what happened to him."

"He was set up you know."

"What makes you so sure Karen?"

"Dating prostitutes wasn't his style Malloy. I'd be more inclined to believe that about you than him. No offense intended of course. Someone planted that stuff on that girl to get him out of the way and it worked. It ruined his career."

"Who would do that to him?" said Malloy.

"Come on detective, a lot of people didn't care for him, especially the bad guys. I thought he was ok. In his younger days, he tried to hard to be a player but that's just a male flaw. How could you blame him for that?"

"So Karen, is he off the force or not?"

"Officially, he's on Malloy because "officially" the department is still investigating the prostitute issue however, the department hasn't issued the poor guy a check in over eight months, so I'd have to say if an employer hasn't paid an employee in that length of time, "I'd say he's off the force.

"Unofficially of course."

"I'd like to meet him."

"You and Warren Gray in the same room... Now that would be like water and oil. Malloy, I'm afraid that the two just don't mix."

"You set it up Karen. I know you can make this happen. Tell him to meet me a Geotona's restaurant over on Red Lion Road on Thursday at 6:00p.m., my treat."

"Your treat...? I might just show up myself. I'll see what I can do."

"Thanks Karen, I knew I could count on you."

"What going on Malloy? It's not like you to come out of your wallet."

"I'm not sure Karen but if my hunch pans out this is going to be the biggest story to hit the Island in a very long time. I have to go Karen. I'll talk to you later."

"Rich here comes that police Sergeant again. I'm going to get some lunch at the Chinese place around the corner."

"Good bring me back some sesame chicken."

"Good morning Sergeant Malloy. How are you today?"

"I'm fine Rich. Can I get a grape soda?"

"Sure you probably need something to wash down all those sunflower seeds."

"How's business going since you opened the garage?"

"Oh it's steady. I just wish the customers would stop scaring my help with all those ghost stories about this place."

"What kind of ghost stories?"

"You tell me Sergeant…you were around here when the murders were committed weren't you?"

"I only know of one murder unless you are talking about the fellow that died in the garage. Everyone called him the gas attendant."

"Tell me about him and don't leave out anything."

"His name was Aubrey. He was well liked."

"How long did he work here?"

"He worked here for about five years. Everyone brought their car to him to be fixed. Sometimes the people would have to wait longer because he had so many customers but they didn't mind the wait because they knew their car would be fixed correctly."

"How did he die?"

"Well...that's still a bit of a mystery. It was ruled an accident but I still have my doubts."

"What happened?"

"Well Aubrey was working late one night and it appeared that the jack slipped from under the car and crushed him. It was the next morning before anyone noticed. The rescue workers removed the car off him and it wasn't a pretty sight. The poor guy's face had been crushed beyond recognition. His family came and claimed the body the next day and took him back to Wyoming where he was buried."

"That's a sad story Sergeant but at least it puts to bed these rumors about him being buried here."

"Who said he was buried here?"

"Some older gentleman that stopped here for gas earlier. He really scared Resa with talk about the garage being the gas attendant's resting place."

"Well now Rich, Aubrey was an Indian and many people, "not just Indians," believe that where an Indian dies is indeed his final resting place. Many people might even see opening the garage as disturbing his resting place. There were rumors for a while after he died that this place was haunted and a lot of people wanted to destroy it."

"Do you mean burn it to the ground? I heard that someone tried to do just that but someone stopped them."

"Yeah...Rich someone did stop them. They say it was Aubrey. Now I wasn't here at the time but some of those people knew the gas attendant well and they say he stopped them even though he had died three days earlier. My father was one of those people."

"Your father...?"

"Yes me Pops worked this area. He was even investigating the murder that took place here before he died."

"How did he die?"

"His car exploded but I don't really feel like talking about it right now. Maybe someday I'll tell you the whole story but not today."

"Ok I look forward to that story. So let's get back to the Gas attendant crap because now I'm confused. You said that they tried to burn the place down three days after he died and someone else said it was three days after Arnold's wife and her lover were killed. Some one else said it was after Mr. Sanford found his wife and her lover dead. Which is true?"

"He came back every time Rich."

"Do you believe that Sergeant?"

"Let me have another soda and yes I believe every word." Don't worry Rich. He could be a friendly ghost, ha ha."

"Not funny Sergeant. Why are you here to-day? Before you answer, I haven't heard from Mr. Sanford's family and I'm starting to doubt that I ever will."

"I understand Rich. How is Old man San-ford doing anyway?"

"There has been no change. A coma is a hard thing to understand."

"You're right about that Richie and thanks for the sodas. How much I owe you?"

"It's on the house this time Sergeant."

"Well thank you Rich and if you happen to see the gas attendant, tell him that I said hi... ha ha."

"Goodbye Sergeant and by the way we have a telephone here, "it might save you some time if you called before you came."

"No I enjoy stopping by. Besides, I'm trying to work up my nerves to ask that mechanic of yours, if she'll have dinner with me. It saddens me that she disappears every time I stop by. I'm starting to believe that she doesn't like me. She's a pretty little thing. You should try to get her to take off those pants and put on a nice dress, get some of that oil and dirt from under her fingernails. Ask her why she doesn't like me. Do you think she's afraid of me?"

"That can't be it Malloy. She just went to get us some Chinese for lunch. I've got a customer. You have a good day."

"Ok Rich, I'll talk to you later."

Chapter 12

"I can't believe we are back at this hospital Rich.

"I'm sorry Resa but we have to do this."

"This crazy shit has to stop Rich. I'm not doing this again and I mean it!"

"I understand why you hate doing this. I will not ask you to do this again Resa, I promise."

"What is it that you want me to do this time?"

"Just go into the room again and check on him."

"Ok but I'll be back in 5 minutes."

"Hello nurse I would like to see my father. His name is Sanford."

"Just a moment."

"Nurse Thomas, someone is here about the deceased gentleman that was in a coma."

"Well it's about time! I'll be there in a few minutes."

"Please have a seat. Nurse Thomas will be here in a few seconds."

"Hello, my name is Yolanda Thomas. Are you Mr. Sanford's daughter?"

"Yes I am."

"What's your name?" "Excuse me...I said what's your name?"

"It's Teresa."

"Please follow me Teresa."

"What's going on? I simply want to see my dad."

"Please have a seat Teresa. I'm afraid that your dad passed away two days ago. Didn't your sister tell you? We tried the contact number that we have on file but no one answered."

"You're telling me that he is dead!"

Yes, "I'm sorry." He wasn't doing well after your sister came to visit him that day. His heart rate had decreased and it finally gave out on him."

"Wait just a minute. Did you just say that my sister was here.... when?"

"She was here the day that he passed away. She had been here most of the day."

"I'm sorry but I have to go."

"Wait you can't leave...what about his arrangements? Teresa come back!"

Teresa ran as fast as she could, in her fright she ran down the wrong corridor twice before finding the correct exit.

"Resa what's wrong?"

"He's dead Rich!"

"What...!?"

"Your boss is dead. He died two days ago. I thought you called to check on him everyday."

"I did the first two weeks but I had stopped calling so much lately. I didn't see much use in it."

"We better get out of here!"

"Wait Resa, I should go in and talk to them."

"You go right ahead and say hi to his daughter when she comes back."

"His daughter...?"

"Yes...the nurse said that his daughter was here the day that he died."

"She spent most of the day with him and later that day he had a heart attack and died. Now please get me out of here Rich, before someone starts asking me, "his daughter" a lot of questions!"

"Ok Resa, "you're right." I wonder why his daughter hasn't been back."

"There are suddenly a lot of unanswered questions Rich. Where is she now and how long has she been here? Why hasn't she come by the station? Damn it! Do you think the bitch is at his house?

"Slow down Resa! Now give me a second to think. Those are all good questions and I think we had better get some answers quickly. I think I should start by calling Elizabeth as soon as we get back to the station. Just relax, once we get back to the garage, I'll get us some answers. I have a question for you Resa. Why do you always disappear when Sergeant Malloy comes around?"

"Because he's the law. Didn't I tell you about the Ohio thing? I need a drink Rich, hurry up and get to the garage. Is this as fast as this thing will go?"

"We'll be there in ten minutes, just enjoy the ride!"

Hello...

"Hello my name is Richard Newell. May I speak to your wife, Elizabeth?"

"She's not here at the moment. This is her husband how may I help you?"

"Well, it's a little complicated but I work for her father. I'm afraid that he died two days ago."

"Mr. Newell is this some kind of sick joke? My wife's father died over twenty years ago."

Yes, "that's what she told me."

"Do you mind if I ask you how he died."

"I guess it can't do any harm if I tell you. He was shot in the face with a shot gun. It was a closed casket funeral because he wasn't recognizable."

"Who shot him?"

"His mistress, I think." Now I'm afraid that's all I can tell you about him."

"Where is Elizabeth now?"

"I'm sorry but I can't tell you that."

"That's fine but according to a nurse at the hospital here on Long Island your wife was here visiting her father two days ago."

"That's impossible! My wife is in New Jersey attending a family member's funeral."

"Who is the family member?"

"Some distant relative, I'm not sure. Now if you will excuse me I'm about to have dinner with my daughter."

"What's your daughter's name?"

"This is the last question that I'm going to answer Mr. Newell. Her name is Lizzy. She was named after her grandmother."

"Sir, I don't want to alarm you but I don't think your wife is being honest with you. I have worked for a man named Sanford for the past two years. He died two days ago. In his house I found the phone number to your house and your wife's name."

"Something about this whole matter is alarming and a lot of lies are being told. If you speak to your wife please ask her to contact me at this number. 631-555-8077, if she is indeed Mr. Sanford's daughter we have a lot to discuss."

"When I talk to her, I will definitely mention my conversation with you. Otherwise, unless she contacts you, please do not call here again Mr. Newell!"
Click...

"He hung up on me Resa. I don't think he knows what his wife is up to or who she really is. He claims that she is in Jersey attending a funeral.

"Maybe it's not her Rich."

"Resa, it's her but why is she being so secretive about who she is?"

"Rich this is New York, people lie all the time. Maybe she has one of those well to do white collar husbands and she doesn't want him to know that she is the daughter of a man who is dirt poor making a living owning a gas station."

"It can't be that simple Resa."

"What are you going to do about your boss? He deserves a decent funeral."

"I'll make sure he gets one Resa but I'm afraid that means another trip to his house."

"What are we looking for this time?"

"His burial papers"

"What if his daughter is there?"

"Actually Resa, "that would be a good thing." Maybe we can find out what she plans to do with this place."

"Where are you going?"

"To Mr. Sanford's home and no you can't go. Stay here and try to make us some money, I get the feeling that we are going to be unemployed very soon."

"Please Rich take me with you, I can't stay here by myself this place is too spooky."

"Oh there you go again. There is nothing spooky about this place. Now stay here, lock the door if you feel safer but you have to stay.

'Locking the door isn't going to make me feel safer, "unless I'm on the outside."

Chapter 13

I was somewhat ashamed of the fact that I hadn't shed a single tear for Mr. Sanford. Maybe the tears would come later. I knew that I had to go to his house and find his insurance papers. On the drive to his house I called the hospital and they confirmed that he had passed away of a heart attack two days ago. I informed them that I would be in touch with them as soon as I could.

When I approached his house I could see that every light in the place was on. I drove up to the drive way. There was a black Ford Taurus parked in front of the house.

I knew the person in that house was his daughter. A part of me thought this was a good thing but another part of me was terrified by what this meant.

I knocked on the front door but there was no answer. I walked around to the back door and knocked but there was no answer. I took out my cell phone and called the number in the house. I could hear the phone ringing but no one was answering.

Maybe she was in the bathroom. So I waited on the front porch for a few minutes and then I knocked again.

There was no answer.

Suddenly there was a voice coming from behind me and it nearly gave me a heart attack. I turned quickly and saw a ghostly elderly lady with a head full of grey hair leaning on a cane.

"What are you doing here?" she snapped with her weak raspy voice.

After I regained my composure, I introduced myself.

"Hello my name is Rich. I work for Mr. Sanford. I was hoping that I might speak to his daughter."

"Sanford doesn't have any daughter."

"Who are you?"

"My name is Rochelle Cromwell. Sanford and I have been neighbors for nearly forty years and if he'd had a daughter, I'd know about it."

"Yes I'm sure that you would, however he does have a daughter but they weren't close. They hadn't been for some time now."

"You are a liar young man! Now I'm asking you for the last time, what are you doing here?"

"Like I said earlier, I'm hoping to speak to his daughter. She is inside the house right now but she's not answering the door."

"No one is inside that house son. I turned on all the lights myself yesterday when Sanford asked me to."

"What did you say?"

"I said I turned on the lights because Sanford asked me to."

"That's impossible, Mr. Sanford passed away two days ago so it isn't possible that you spoke to him."

"He spoke to me in my dreams. He asked me to do one last favor for him and it was to turn on all the lights in the house. Now if I were you young man I would get back to where ever you came from!"

"Miss Cromwell, I'm trying to get his burial papers together so I can make sure he has a proper burial!"

"That's no concern of yours. Besides, it's already taken care of. I suggest that you get back to where you came from! And I also suggest that you call a taxi to take you there." You should not be driving that car! You don't know what you have done by removing it from that garage!

"I know that it was probably wrong for me to take his car but I'm the only one that could take care of his station and I needed that car to do it."

"Well maybe you could get away with that while he was in the hospital but now that he has passed away you should return all his property."

"The car is the only thing that I have of his."

"What about his keys?"

"Well I still need the keys."

"You don't need the ones to his house, give them to me!"

"Why should I give them to you?"

"Because I say you should and if you don't there will be some jail time for you to pay!

"Listen Lady, you are starting to get on my last nerves. I normally wouldn't speak to my elders this way but some strange stuff is going on around here and I'm about ready to get to the bottom of it!" Now, I'm not denying that you are his friend but right now the only thing I care about is getting inside that house and talking to his daughter."

"I just told you that he doesn't have a daughter."

"Well whose car is that?"

"The woman that was driving that car returned to her home yesterday."

"Well that looks like a rental car. Why would she leave it here?"

"Maybe she had to leave in a hurry. Which was probably a good idea, "apparently she was a lot smarter than you are!"

"Why would she be here if she wasn't his daughter? I know for a fact that she was at the hospital checking on him. I know that she is his daughter and I'm not going anywhere until I speak to her!"

"For the last time Mr. Newell, "she is not his daughter." Now I don't care if you use to work for Sanford, give me the keys to his car and get the hell away from my friend's house!"

"I'm not going anywhere!"

"Fine you stupid, stupid man! You just stay right there while I go call the police and tell them what you've been up to."

"Alright...

"Can you at least call me a taxi?"

"There's one on the way, he should be here any second...

༄

"Hi Rich I didn't hear you drive up."

"That's because I was walking Resa. I only had enough money on me to pay the taxi driver to drop me off two blocks away."

"What are you talking about? Did something happen to the car?

"No nothing happened to the car. I went to Mr. Sanford's house and his neighbor made me give her the keys to the car."

"You gave our car away?"

"Resa...calm down. First of all, it wasn't our car. Mr. Sanford is dead, so we have to make other arrangements. His neighbor claims that they were good friends. She has taken over the place as if it were hers."

"Do you think she is his girlfriend?"

"I don't think so. This woman looks like she's about ninety years old."

"Maybe he likes older women Rich."

"Some men like older women Resa but not thirty years older. Besides, if he had a girlfriend, I think I would have known."

"You never know Rich. The older the better they say. Did you talk to the daughter?"

"That's another thing...the old hag claims the girl is not his daughter. She said that the girl went back home to Tennessee yesterday. I know she's his daughter...I just know it. Her rental car was parked in front of the garage. I think something is going on over there. I want to go back and check things out. That scary ass old woman has turned on every light in the house. She claims that Mr. Sanford spoke to her in her dreams and asked her to do it for him. Something isn't right at all.

"Oh Rich, this is not good. Are we going to lose our jobs?"

"I'm not sure what's going to happen Resa."

"By the way that man came by asking about your pictures...I mean your art. He said it was important for you to call him first thing tomorrow."

"Really...what was he doing out this way at this time of night?"

"Looked like he was headed to a party. He was all dressed up and had a nice looking woman with him. She really had a nice ass on her."

"Resa, why were you looking at her ass?"

"You don't know Rich? After all this time we've been together, you don't know."

"I don't know what Resa? Stop talking in riddles. I've had enough freaking riddles for one night."

"Come on Rich. You are a nice looking man. Haven't you ever wondered why I haven't hit on you?"

"No, I hadn't wondered."

"Well Rich, lets just say that men are not my cup of tea."

"Snap, crackle and pop. Are you telling me that you like women Resa?"

"Heck no Rich! I love me the heck out of a woman. I'm a lesbian. I thought you knew and were being kind by not saying anything."

"Resa are you pulling my leg?"

"No I'm not Rich but if you were a woman I'd be pulling on it right now."

"I think I better go outside Resa. I need to think and you are really screwing up my head now. Do you really like women? Never mind…

"Good evening detective Warren Gray."

"Hello Sergeant Malloy. What is this little get together about?"

"Well Gray, I just wanted to know what you've got up your sleeves. "

What are you talking about?"

"I think that you and I are after the same thing and I think we might be able to solve this little mystery quicker if we worked together."

"No thanks Malloy. I work alone."

"I knew that would be you answer. Let me ask you something Gray. For years you have been beating the streets making a name for yourself. Things were going very well for you until that little mishap with the prostitute over in Brooklyn last year. Most people think that you are guilty but there are a few people that think that you were set up. I'm one of those people. I'm retiring in a few years but before I do, I'd really like to solve the mystery surrounding that spooky gas station over on 19th and Clover."

"What mystery are you talking about Malloy?"

"You know very well what I'm talking about. There are some things that just don't add up."

"What things?"

"The daughter is a mystery. Where is she? It just doesn't make any sense. Her father is a coma and no one has heard anything from her."

"Well Malloy according to that gas attendant they weren't very close. So if they haven't been talking all these years, what makes you think she would be calling to check on him the last couple of weeks?"

"That's just it Gray. Someone might have been able to contact her but she doesn't want anyone to know that she is the daughter. Sounds crazy I know but it's the only thing that makes sense to me. My question is why? Also there were some papers missing from the files. Do you know anything about that? Please don't insult my intelligence by lying to me Gray."

"Ok Malloy, I took the missing files." What are you going to do about it?"

"I don't plan to do anything as long as you cooperate with me. Now the way I see it, if we share information with each other right now we might be able to solve this ghostly mystery very soon. First I want you to tell me everything that you have uncovered so far. After you do that, "I'll tell you everything that I know."

"No freaking way Malloy. Who told you, I was that stupid!"

"No one had to tell me Gray and I'm not saying that you are stupid."

"Well then how about you giving me all your information first and then I'll decide if I want to share my information with you."

"Screw you Gray. You really are an asshole. This meeting is…

"Hold on one minute Malloy, let me answer my cell phone."

Hello…

"Gray, it's Stephanie."

"Hi…what's up?"

"I got that information that you asked for."

"Great let me have it."

"Ok…but you're not going to believe what I found out."

"Sure I will, let me have it."

"Gray all these people are deceased."

"Are you sure?"

"I triple checked it Gray."

"Ok, thanks for your help."
"Gray...

"Yes sweetheart."

"This is some scary stuff...

"Yeah I know. Thanks, I owe you and your old man a dinner at Fredica's."

"That won't be necessary Gray...but if you want to meet me alone tomorrow for drinks, "I'm up for that."

"Really..? Ok, just tell me when and where."

"I'll call you back in a few minutes."

"Malloy, I think we are about to enter into a partnership but first I think we better order a couple of drinks, I feel like celebrating."

"Make mine a tall Long Island Ice Tea."

"I just got some news that you are not going to believe...

"Try me…"

Chapter 14

I went back to the house after midnight. The lights were all still on. I didn't see either car. For some reason this terrified me. I stood outside the house near the hedges and watched to see if there was any movement. There was none.

Just to make sure that the old lady didn't sneak up on me again I decided to check out her house also. All of her lights were out except for the one in her garage. I found an old chair and climb up to look inside the window of her garage. For the most part it was neat. There was a small car in the center of the garage with a car cover over it. I surveyed the remainder of the garage and then my eyes went back to the car.

Even though it was covered, I knew the shape of that car! It was a Porsche! Probably my Porsche! I was excited and pissed off at the same time. Then I thought back to the first conversation that I had with Sergeant Malloy. He was right after all.

How could Mr. Sanford do this to me? I had to sit down for a few minutes and gather my thoughts. Maybe just maybe, it wasn't my car but I knew in my heart that it was. It was all so clear to me now. Mr. Sanford had insisted that I get him the title to the car which I did. He said that the people in the junkyard wouldn't take the car without it. I was suddenly furious.

An hour had passed. It was time for me to try a window to get into his house. I got lucky. The window at the rear of the house was unlocked. I climbed through the window and quietly closed it.

After I took three steps inside the house I was horrified as all the lights went out. I started sweating profusely. I could tell I was not alone.

I felt the same presence that I had felt on my first trip inside this house five weeks ago, only this time whatever it was didn't try to leave the house.

This time it stood its ground.

For some reason I decided to speak.

"Hello...I heard my trembling voice say."

"Hello Rich was the terrifying reply. What in the name of all that's right in this world are you doing in my house boy?"

"Who are you? Is that you Mr. Sanford?"

"Who I am...is of no concern to you boy. Why are you in this house?"

"I'm looking for something...something very important."

As the dim light from the outside started to slowly fill the dark room I could see two forms standing less than ten feet away from me. Neither was human but then again maybe both were.

Suddenly there was a tightness in my chest and I found myself gasping for air. It was obvious that whatever was in the room with me was aware of my plight.

Before I knew it I was on my knees looking up at the faceless creatures that were about to take my life

I heard a voice say.

"You should leave the house and the gas station Rich and never return. Do you understand?"

"Shut up woman replied another voice. I'll handle this."

"Mr. Richard Newell, I believe it's time for you to find another job. You have done a fairly good job so far but it is indeed time that you leave the station. Have I made myself clear? Do you understand?"

I didn't understand but I could not speak to say I didn't understand. That voice sounded a lot like Mr. Sanford but I knew it couldn't be because he was dead. My mind didn't want to understand anything anymore, all it wanted was for me to get out of that house and never return.

I could dimly see the outline of the back door and I tried to get to my feet and run to it but my legs felt as though they were weighed down with cement. It seemed the closer I got to the door the heavier the presence in the room became.

I reached out and grabbed for the door knob but something spun me around like I was a rag doll in a typhoon.

Get out of this house and never return is all I remember hearing. The door flung open and I found myself flying through the night air onto the ground on the outside of the house. I landed on my hand and I heard a snap but I felt no pain.

Suddenly there was a loud boom and all the lights came on inside the house again. I jumped up off the ground without looking back and ran for my life...

When I finally got back to the station there were no sign of Resa and all my art was missing. Things were happening too fast. I knew I couldn't stay inside this gas station for a split second more. I rushed behind the counter and opened the secret compartment.

Could this night get any worse? All the money was gone. Every cent that we had made the past four weeks was gone…even the picture of the beautiful girl was gone. None of this made any sense.

I heard a car and looked out the window. It was the Chevy! It was parked outside the garage. Suddenly, the garage door slowly started to open. I stood there once again unable to move as I watched the Chevy slowly pull into the garage.

How was this happening? My mind just couldn't comprehend what my eyes were seeing. There was no driver! The door to the garage slowly started to close but there was no one there.

My heart was pounding so hard that I knew my life would be over in just a few seconds. I fell onto the floor where I had waited on hundreds of customers over the past two years. As I slowly drifted into the world of the unknown I thought I heard Resa say…

"Aubrey I really liked this one. It's a shame he had to die. He was only trying to help us."

A voice answered and said Lilly, "I liked him too but he was getting too close to the truth. We can not allow him or anyone else to disturb our burial ground. Now help me put him in the car. His time here is over."

Good bye Rich...said the spirit that he knew in her human form as Resa but in her world was known as Lilly. Maybe someday in the after life we will meet and we can once again be friends. Don't worry about your art either. I have a feeling that it's going to be worth something real soon.

"Don't worry Lilly. He to will be one of us because he is also a gas attendant. Now I think it's time for you to get back home to your family in Tennessee."

"Of course you're right Aubrey. They must be getting worried."

"Don't worry about the station or your father's house. I will keep an eye on both."

"What about the Chevy Aubrey? Do you really plan to destroy it?"

"Yes...someday. If I hadn't been trying to repair the brakes on it that night I might still be alive."

"It's not the car's fault Aubrey. You were tired and it was late. You should not have been working so late. I think it's time that you released the curse. It's not fair that everyone who drives it dies."

"First of all, I wasn't tired. I had just replaced the front grill. It was damaged when someone backed into it. The grill was from a 57 Chevy. I guess that why people kept getting confused about what year it was. I was also under the car checking the brake lines. I thought I heard someone come in...the next thing that I knew the car was on top of me."

"So it really wasn't an accident."

"No, it wasn't an accident! I knew the sound of those footsteps. It was a woman with high heel shoes. It was your mother Lilly. Your mother pulled the safety off the jack and the car fell."

"Why would she do that?"

"I threatened to tell on her. She was always bringing some man to the garage and taking him to the room over the garage. I was tired of it because your father had always been good to me. He knew about his unfaithful wife but he still loved her. That's what really drove him insane not her death. Your mother was a beautiful woman Lilly and she loved that red dress that your father had bought her for Valentine's Day in 1953 but she couldn't be satisfied with just one man. Time after time she would wear that red dress for other men. They would climb those stairs to the room over this garage and shortly after that they would leave. I know this is probably not easy for you to hear but some nights there would be as many as four men making that trip up those stairs."

"I find it hard to believe that my mother could be that way but then again I never knew her. Why haven't you told me this story before?"

"I didn't know how to. It's in the past now. We need to concentrate on the present. Now pull the Chevy outside Lilly and lets chain the garage door locked again. I'll ask your uncle Harry to drive it back to the house as soon as he's back from visiting your father at the Asylum. This time I'll make sure that no one can drive it again."

"There's just one more question Aubrey."

"What is it Lilly?"

"Were you one of her lovers?"

"That's a fair question but the answer is no. She approached me several times but I refused her every time. It was after that they she started seeing more and more men. I think she wanted to hurt me."

"Why would she want to hurt you?"

"It's simple, I loved your father more than I loved her."

"So you had feeling for my mom?"

"Yes Lilly I loved her. I loved her with all my heart and soul and she knew it. The first time I saw her in that red dress, I wanted her so bad. I even followed her upstairs one night when your father was away. As she lay there on that bed with the gray silk sheets and that red dress with her beautiful legs exposed, she was really something to behold but I couldn't do that to your father and she hated me for it. After that night she made my life a "living nightmare" around here."

"I'm glad you told me about this Aubrey."

"So am I Lilly."

"What are we going to do about detective Gray and Sergeant Malloy?"

"Nothing Lilly, it will be fun to see how close they come to the truth." Besides, they can't harm us, we're already dead."

"Ok Aubrey, until next time and we both know there will be a next time."

"Lilly there's just one thing. That picture of you and your parents should stay locked away. Every time you look at it something happens. I want you to find peace and it will never happen unless you let what happened to you that night rest."

"I can't Aubrey. He was my uncle and I loved him. How could he do that to me?"

"He was drunk Lilly. He thought you were his wife."

"That was no reason to kill me. I was only eleven years old. How could he (sob) mistake me for her?"

"Some things are hard to explain Lilly. I don't believe he meant to kill you but after he did he felt that he had to cover it up. The death of you and your mother was only a few days apart." Your father was already suffering so much. Harry knew this would push him over the edge. Twins share a stronger bond than most siblings. They can feel each other's pain." So he had your father committed to the Asylum and with you out of the way he just assumed your father's identity. No one was the wiser."

"But I'm not really dead Aubrey."

"That's correct Lilly. I'm afraid that you are in a far worst place. You are in between and until you completely cross over you will never find peace and neither will your human counter part Teresa. Both of you need rest.

"Who is that? I see car lights."

"It's that detective and Sergeant Malloy."

"What are they doing?"

"They have gas cans!"

"They are going to burn down the garage."

"Quick pull the car out. If we don't get that car out we won't be able to stop them....

"Aubrey, they are blocking the garage door with his car!"

"Well...it looks like they aren't giving me a choice. I'll have to kill them too. I can't allow anyone to disturb our burial ground."

"No Aubrey, let them do it."

"Now why would I do that?"

"So I can be free...

"What about your husband and daughter?

"They will be free also. Free from all the lies and deceit that I brought into their life."

"I'm sorry Lilly but I can't allow that to happen."

"It's already happening. If the Chevy burns, so does your spirit and mine. Aubrey you have protected this place long enough. It's time to let them have it!"

"No, no, no, I will not!"

"It's too late Aubrey or have you forgotten about Rich's body. Your powers are limited in this place with a human body that hasn't crossed over yet and there are two of us. Rich and I (sob) have not crossed over. I'm afraid that the only one that can save this place tonight is me."

"What can you do Lilly?"

"I can go outside and introduce myself to the two gentleman and hope that they are willing to listen to reason. I think one of them has been looking for me for a very long time."

"It's not going to work Lilly but I see your mind is made up."

"Promise me that you will stay inside Aubrey. Promise me...

"I can't promise that but go ahead and handle things your way."

"Hello Sergeant Malloy...

"Who are you and how do you know my name?"

"Hello detective Gray."

"Hello Elizabeth or do you prefer Lilly?"

"Who is she Gray?"

"Don't you know Malloy? You've only been looking for her about fifty years now. This my friend...is the daughter of Harold Sanford. She's your missing daughter."

"I don't understand. This woman can't be over thirty-years old."

"That because she isn't human, at least not completely."

"Where have you been?"

"I'm sorry Sergeant but that is privileged information."

"That's fine but I'm going to have to ask you to step aside."

"I will do no such thing. I can't let you burn down my father's place." Do I smell alcohol? You gentleman should go home and try to sleep this off before you do something that you might regret. How is it going to look in the paper today when you are arrested for arson?"

"Elizabeth this is not something that we want to do but you know we must. We can no longer allow you and others like you to exist here."

"I strongly hope that you gentlemen change your minds quickly."

"Where is Rich?" said Malloy.

"I'm afraid he is no longer with us. He had a heart attack shortly after midnight."

"Are you saying that he is dead?" said Malloy.

"I'm afraid so," said Lilly.

"How did he die? Did you kill him? He was a good kid. He didn't deserve to die. I demand to know what happened to him. Where is his body? Did he die here and if so where is the ambulance?"

"I just told you he had a heart attack now Sir. You are asking too many questions. It would be in your best interest to get in you car and go home"

"I'm not going anywhere until I find out what happen to Rich. Now what really happened to him! Where is that mechanic?"

"She ran off with all the money and his art. It was pretty sad actually but she won't get far, I promise you that."

"Listen to me Elizabeth! We have to burn this place down. There are too many mysteries associated with this place. The few old people from the old neighborhood have spoken. They want to see this place burned to the ground and so do I!"

"Where are these people that you speak of detective Gray?" said Lilly.

"They are not here tonight but I speak for all of them."

"If I were you detective, I would just go home and try to sober up. We have done no wrong here. Give Stephanie a call maybe she will stop by and you can work on killing her also with that second hand smoke from your cigarettes."

"Now I'm only going to say this once. Get back in your car and leave this place. If you ever come by here again, Aubrey and I will make sure that you don't leave here alive. Do you understand me?"

"Malloy what are you doing?"

"Something that I should have done a long time ago. Let's burn it to the ground Gray. Let's do it now!"

"I'm warning you to stop! Put down the gas cans. Get in your car and leave this place and never return!"

"Oh my God! Who are you?" said Gray.

"Tell him who I am Malloy."

"I see you but I can't believe my own eyes. It's Aubrey. All the rumors are true. He's the mechanic that died here almost fifty years ago. Until now I thought is was just a crazy rumor. We better do as he says Gray. Come on lets get far, far away from here before it's too late!"

"Get in your car and leave gentlemen and don't you ever come back. If you do I promise you that you will not leave here alive."

"Let's go Gray, let's go now! You drive Gray my hands are shaking so badly that I won't be able to hold the steering wheel. How in the world did I let you talk me into coming here in the first place? It had to be that dang Long Island Ice tea. One of the first things that me Pops taught me was to never drink on the job… now I understand what he meant."

"Which one Malloy? You had half a dozen but if you were half the man that your father was those couple of drinks would not have you acting like a little girl!"

"I guess it was the last one. Come on lets get out of here before I completely lose what's left of my senses. One last thing Gray, don't you ever compare me and my Pops, again...do you understand me? You washed up detective!"

"Well, it looks like they came to their senses Aubrey."

"Don't be so sure about that Lilly. I have a feeling that they will be back. I wish I was wrong but I just know they will. These humans are the worst kind. I think Malloy is ok for the most part but I saw something in detective Gray's eyes that teetered on the verge of insanity. He will be a problem."

"Yes, maybe you're right, I saw it too. He has a wish that may never be granted. He will continue to come back until he gets what he wants regardless of the consequences."

"Unfortunately, I agree."

"Aubrey hurry and pull the car out of the garage. We need to get Rich to the house quickly. It's not too late for him. We can still savage something good from this night, if we act quickly."

"I'm going back Malloy."

"Going back where?"

"To the Garage and I'm going to burn it to the ground."

"Don't be a fool Gray. You stupid idiot turn this car around now! We have to take a couple of days and think things through with clear minds. We need a fool proof plan."

"No...I'm burning that place to the ground tonight. If you want out of the car open the door and jump out now."

"You're going too fast for me to jump you stupid drunk idiot! How do you plan to burn that place down? They took the gas can! This is crazy Gray, lets just go home and sober up like the stupid girl said."

"What girl? Do you mean that spirit? She's not human Malloy. Couldn't you see how the street light was glowing right through her?"

"I admit there was some strange glow about her but I thought that I had just had one too many Long Island Ice Teas. Now are you going to turn this car around or do I have to take out my pistol and whip your ass with it?"

"Ha, ha, you just sit over there on your side old man and watch as I make history."

"I still don't see how we can do anything without gas."

"Don't worry about gas. There is plenty in the tank of this car. All we have to do is run this car into the garage and the station will go up in smoke when the car hits it."

"What about us? You stupid moron!"

"We can jump out just before the car hits. There's the garage now."

"Please Gray stop the car now. You've had too much to drink!" "You're not thinking straight."

"I'm thinking just as straight as your old man was when he tried to burn the place down all those years ago. You didn't think I knew about that did you?"

"Me Pops did no such thing! Now stop this funky smelling car or I swear I'll but a bullet in your leg right now."

"You don't have the nerve old man. We are about to make history. Just think, we will be the ones who finally put an end to it all."

"Gray stop the car!"

"I'm not stopping. If you want out you better jump out now."

"I'm trying but I can't get my door open."

"What are you talking about Malloy?"

"My door won't open!"

"Neither will mine!" shouted Gray.

"Oh dear God…hit the brakes fool!"

"I am but they are not working! The accelerator is stuck…

Just as the car went through the garage door, Malloy and Gray saw Elizabeth, Aubrey and Rich standing in front of the garage door. The car went through them and the garage door then quickly burst into flames as it hit the rear of the 56Chevy.

The three gas attendants sadly but quickly put out the fire. The image of the terrified men faces as the car crashed into the building would forever be etched in their minds. Afterwards, Lilly called the Police and the fire department. It was too late to call an ambulance."

The next day a new garage door was installed. The door was chained, never to be opened again. Rich hung a sign on the door. It read…HELP WANTED no mechanic needed.

The following week one brand new "old style" gas pump was installed. The color was red. It was a perfect match for the newly painted building.

Parked outside the station was a shiny red 1982 Porsche. It had brand new seats and a new more powerful engine. Rich used it everyday to drive to his new home that he shared with his new landlords the Sanfords.

Occasionally, when the wind blew just right, there would be a heavy scent of Detective's Gray's cologne in the air. At other times there would be a small trail of sunflower seeds leading from the pumps to the garage door.

Every year on the eve of the crash. Rich would see Sergeant Malloy and Detective Gray's ghostly forms standing near the gas pumps with gas cans in their hands, looking in the direction of the station. They both had determined looks on their faces but never came closer than the pumps.

Rich felt sorry for them. It was obvious that they had not crossed over. They probably never would unless they gave up the crazy notion of burning down the station. As long as I here that will never happen thought Rich. It's like Aubrey said…"We can not allow anyone to destroy our burial ground!"

The End

Bonus material: "19th and Clover"
Book 2 of "The Gas Attendant"

Introduction

"Good morning Herman. I made some coffee. Did you sleep well?"

"Yes I did Lilly."

"What are you planning to do on your day off?"

"I thought I would just kick back and enjoy a good movie. Where is Elizabeth?"

"She's over at the neighbor's house playing with Merissa."

"Isn't it too early to be bothering the neighbors that way?"

"Not really, the truth is she spent the night over there."

"Oh yeah…and why wasn't I aware of that?"

"Well…I was going to tell you but you got home so late. I also had something on my mind that I really needed to talk to you about." I chickened out at the last minute but I fear I must tell you now."

"Lilly you seem so serious. What is wrong baby?"

"I don't know where to start. That's not true, I know exactly where to start but I need you to know that I love you and Lizzy with all my heart and soul. I fear you will leave me after you have heard what I have to say."

"Honey calm down. Nothing you can say would make me want to leave you. Whatever it is, we will find a way to work through it.

Herman stared at his wife. She was indeed worried about something. He had never seen her this way before. When Lilly spoke her eyes filled with tears and her lips trembled. Herman grabbed her and held her tightly as she spoke.

"I have been lying to you since day one. I'm not (sob) who you think I am.

"Really…who are you?"

"I'm a ghost…or a more correct term would be a spirit," said Lilly.

"Ha, ha, ha…oh Lilly you had me going for a second there. Woman what in the world has made you come up with such a tale?"

"I'm not joking! When I was eleven years old my uncle came into my room and he raped me! He was drunk and thought I was his wife. By the time he realized what he had done, it was too late. I was just a child and my mother had just died a few days earlier. The trauma of what I had just been through had rendered me unconscious. He thought I was dead. Instead of taking me to the hospital he attempted to bury my body at the homestead on the eastside of Long Island, New York. He was so drunk that he passed out before he finished digging the grave.

When I finally woke, my body was wrapped in an old quilt. My uncle was lying on the cold ground beside me fast asleep. I tried to wake him but it was useless. I was freezing. It was mid January. All I had on was my pajamas. I went next door and rang the doorbell. It was almost three o'clock in the morning. An elderly gray haired woman answered the door and was not happy that someone was waking her up so early. When she saw me, she gasped as if she had seen an old friend but a friend that should not be here and more importantly not in the dire state that I was. She quickly surveyed the surrounding and ushered me inside her home where I collapsed in front of her fireplace. Two days later I awoke in her bed.

I surveyed the room. There were candles everywhere and the old lady was on her knees praying in a strange tongue. She stopped suddenly and looked in my direction. She slowly got off her knees and softly said, "it's a miracle! You are back from the dead child. With a smile on her wrinkled face she repeated, "you are back from the dead..."

Chapter 1

"Good morning Rich…how are you today?"

"Hi Grand dad. I'm pretty sore right now. Got stung this morning while I was out in the woods looking for some honey."

"Damn it boy if, I've told you once, I've told you a thousand times. Don't mess with them honey bees unless you have a grown up with you. Now let me see where them bees stung your young stupid ass."

Rich took off his shirt so that his Grand dad could view his backside. The bites hurt more than he would ever admit to.

"Well…that's as bad as I've ever seen. You best stop your painting and come with me, so we can put something on those bites to draw out the infection."

"I'll be right in as soon as I finish with this art piece."

"Ha, ha, you are still calling them paintings art."

"Yes they are art. Lots of people think I should take them to New York and sell them. Maybe, I will do that someday when I'm old enough but I will need to get me a car before that can happen. I believe someone will pay me lots of money for them someday."

"Well…the important thing is that you believe. I won't fault you for that not one little bit. I think it's a great thing for a young person to have a dream. You best hurry though…them bites look mighty nasty."

"I'll be there soon Grand dad."

It was three days before the pain of the bites started to subside. The homemade salve was a great help.

Cleve Evans stood 6 feet 2 inches tall. Farming the land had kept him fit with a slender build and thick muscular arms. He and his wife had lived in

Carolina their entire life. They lived off the land mostly, hunting wild game in the winter and growing a variety of vegetables in the summer. It was a good life.

"Come with me boy, I've got something that I want to show you."

Rich followed his grandfather to the back of the barn. When they got there; a wonderful surprise awaited him.

"Help me get this tarp off the car boy."

"Wow...is this a Porsche Grand dad?"

"Yes it is boy, it's a 1982, Porsche 924. This car saved the company from going bankrupt. I haven't driven her in almost six years. I start her up every few months but I never take her out for a ride anymore. I think we will take her out today."

"I didn't know you had a car like this. It is beautiful but it needs a paint job."

"Yes, I know. Get in boy...lets see if she will move."

The old car started with a rumble and my grand-father was smiling from ear to ear. He put her in first gear and eased off the clutch; the little car jerked and went dead. My grandfather tried again but this time he released the hand brake and the little car took off smoothly. We raced around the country side for a few miles and then back to the barn.

"Well…what do you think boy?"

"That was fun. I felt like we were racing around on the train tracks. Why did we come back so quickly?" said Rich.

"The temperature gauge was too high. I think she has been sitting so long that the ther-mostat is stuck in the open position or the water pump has gone bad. I'll have to check that out later."

"Grand dad…do you mind if I get the water hose and give her a bath?

"Boy, that's a splendid idea. Here's the key. Pull her down to the house and have at it."

"Grand dad, I've never driven a stick before."

"Are you kidding me? Boy when I was your age, I could drive anything. That worthless father of yours never taught you how to drive a stick? That should have been the first thing he taught you to drive in. Oh well...I guess I should not speak ill of the deceased. May he rest in peace. I'll drive her down to the house and once I fix her, I'll teach you how to drive her."

As Rich washed the car, his Grandfather watched him through the kitchen window. The boy loved the car; it was easy to see that. Once he was finished; he stood back and admired his handy work. The little red car now had a new owner, as soon as he taught the boy to drive it; he would hand over the keys to him.

"It looks great boy. I can't ever remember it looking better, not even when it was brand new."

"How much a car like this cost Grand Dad?"

"A lot boy, not really worth what I paid for it...but then what is? I think it's about time to get her back on the road."

"Why did you stop driving it?"

"Well…as I got older, it was harder to get in and out of it. I thought about selling it once or twice but then I would think about all the good times me and your grandmother had in it. We once drove it to the Florida Keys. I had a bike rack on it at the time. I thought it would be a great idea for us to ride around on our bikes once we got there. The bike rack was a great ideal but driving this little car that far was a huge mistake; we were sore for a month. Ha, ha and your Grandmother wouldn't speak to me for at least that long."

"Lol…I guess that was a bad thing huh?"

"Ha, ha, you are too young to understand that but this is a young man's car. It is still a good car. With the right owner it could last a long time yet."

"Gramps you sound like my parents when I used to ask about "baby making weather". I miss them so much."

"I know you do boy. I miss them too. Life is strange that way. I never thought I would out live my son. Listen I was thinking…I'm almost seventy years old. It's time that I got rid of this car."

"No don't do that. It's a beautiful car and you just said it has some good years left in it."

"You're right I did just say that…didn't I? Maybe you're right; I'm just an old man with crazy thoughts…why just a few minutes ago I was thinking about giving this here car to you. Silly of me I know…why you can't even drive the thing."

"What! Are you serious? Oh Grand dad… do you really mean it?"

Rich ran and hugged Old Man Evans tightly. The old man shed a few tears and squeezed his only grand child tightly.

"You are the best Grandfather in the whole world," smiled Rich.

That night Rich stared out his bedroom window at the little red Porsche. He could not believe it actually belonged to him. When he was finally able to sleep, he had a nightmare. It was about the day his parents died. It was only by the grace of God that he survived...the car flipped at least seven times...his father attempted to hold the car steady as the two oncoming trucks raced around the curb. It all happened so fast. In the Carolina Mountains there was no room on the side of the road and it was either run smack dab into the semis or swerve and hope for the best...well the best left him without parents. It had been over a year now but the nightmare would not go away. The truck drivers didn't even stop to help...

(Three billion tears later...)

"Oh Rich please don't stop...it feels so good, said Karen. Please tell me that I will be your only lover from this day until the end of eternity"

"I promise baby, you are so sweet and lovely. You are the cutest virgin in Northport. I wish to never be with another woman. I will teach you all you need to know about the art of love making."

"I look forward to it my love. Now we better get out of this barn before my dad comes home."

'No Karen, not yet. Lets do it one more time."

"Ok Rich but you must promise to leave as soon as we are finished."

"I promise, now remember that thing that I was telling you that I like to do with my tongue…

Yes giggled Karen…"I thought you were just joking about putting your tongue down there. It just seems so nasty."

"It's only nasty if you don't bathe yourself daily. I know how clean you keep yourself. I can smell the sweet honey of your body now."

Ha, ha, "silly man…that is the molasses from the pancake breakfast this morning."

"That's not the smell I'm talking about sexy…now lay back on the hay and relax," said Rich

Karen laid back on the new bed of hay and bit her lips as Rich softly kissed her on the neck and softly sucked the hard nipple on each of her breasts. It felt so good but nothing in her entire life felt as good as the moment he covered her entire vagina with his mouth and slowly started to caress her clit in a circular motion with his tongue. The climax was so intense that she yelled out in joy, she actually cried out so loud that all the birds in the trees in a two mile radius flew away in fear.

Once the wonderful sensation started to subside and she was finally able to move, she looked down at a smiling Rich, as he said...the best is yet to come.

(Two years later)

"Karen are you feeling ok?" said Jackson.

"Sure, I feel just fine. Why do you ask?"

"Well...for the past three days, you have been sitting in that chair staring out toward the North woods. If I were a betting man, I would bet that you are thinking about that young man up there in New York. I still say you should have gone with him."

"No Dad…that was not going to work. Rich is just too much of a dreamer. Besides, he was my first love. Everyone knows you don't run off with your first love. Especially, to a big city like New York."

"Well…suit yourself. Personally, I always liked Rich. He is well mannered and well liked in this part of the woods. Maybe he is somewhat of a dreamer but he is trustworthy and he also has a good heart."

"Yeah dad…I know"

It had been almost a week since Rich loaded up and headed to the Big Apple. Karen was shocked and angry when he gave her the news. When he told her that he wanted to talk to her down by the pond under the tree that they had made love under a hundred times, she knew he was about to ask her to marry him. The news shocked her and she was unable to speak. The silly town folk had filled his head with crazy talk about him selling his art in the Big Apple.

She listened to the dreamer talk about how nice it would be to live in one of those fancy "high rise" apartments in Manhattan. When he asked her to go with him, she hugged him tightly and said she would think about it but she knew she would not be heading to that cold place. She had read about how cold the East Coast winters could be. As soon as she came home that night she went straight to bed and cried herself to sleep.

A few days before he left, the people of Northport, South Carolina, gave him a hero's send off that rivaled any 4th of July celebration that the small town had seen in the last fifty years. As Karen sat in the stands watching the celebration, Mr. Elroy Johnston winked at her as he thought to himself. You are all mine now baby. Karen quickly looked away from the old man that had stumbled upon her one day several years ago as she bathed her eighteen year old body in the pond behind her father's ranch. At that time she was still a virgin. She didn't know exactly how long he had been there gawking at her but she quickly swam to the bank and hurriedly put her clothes on, later she thought maybe letting him see her completely nude was not a smart move. Since that day, he had made many excuses to stop by the ranch.

Sometimes, she hated her father for being so gullible. Why didn't he suspect what that old man was up to? One day as Karen was picking blueberries on the homestead; Mr. Johnston silently rode up behind her on his prized Arabian stallion and made his move. Karen was completely taken off guard and fought the old guy but for some strange reason she didn't fight him long. As he lay on top of her tugging at her blouse, she began to think about how Rich had broken her heart and something inside of her lost it. Suddenly, the woman that had loved only one man her entire life relaxed and welcomed her attacker's advances. A shocked Mr. Johnston could not believe his eyes as the young woman pushed his hands away and tossed her blouse onto the blueberry patch and yelled…you better fuck me good!

As he gazed down at her firm peach size breasts, he finally felt his old stubborn penis come alive…this was a welcomed event for he had not been able to "get it up" for quite a long time. He had thought there was something wrong with him but now he knew the truth.

Mr. Johnston looked down at Karen but she looked away as he entered her young vibrant body. His heart raced out of control as he pumped up and down on the young woman; suddenly he felt her love canal tighten around his cock. He felt like he was an eighteen year old kid again and didn't miss a beat when Karen yelled out fuck me harder Rich. Mr. Johnston was thankful for the Viagra pill that he had taken earlier in the day. So he tried to give her what she asked for and just before he felt his 59 year old heart getting ready to burst through his chest, he felt the young woman squeeze him slightly and was sure he had managed to do something that hadn't happened with his 57 year old wife in over fifteen years...Karen seemed surprised when she came out of her stupor and realized the old man grinning down at her was not Rich.

She jumped up and ran home leaving the blouse in the blueberry patch. Mr. Johnston picked it up, smelled it deeply and thought... Yes, you are mine now...

"Karen…What the hell are you doing shouted her mom! Where is your blouse? Where are the berries for the pie?"

"Please mom (sob) not right now. Please… just don't talk to me right now?"

Karen's mom just stood there in shock looking out toward the blueberry patch. She wasn't sure but it looked like she saw a horse in the distant patch. She didn't have on her glasses so she could not be sure… What had startled her daughter…more importantly where was her blouse..?

Karen turned on the shower and welcomed the warm water against her skin. What had she done? How could she lose control like that? She scrubbed her skin hoping to wash away the filth of the old man's touch…it did no good. She cussed the name Richard Newell.

Chapter 2
(three weeks later)

"Good morning Arnold, how was your night?" said Rich.

"Morning son, it was a pretty long one. The only company I had was that damn Alley Cat across the way. He was chasing those freaking mice all night. He finally caught one around 3:00am. I'm ready for some shut eye. Tell Old man Sanford that I took in a total of forty-seven dollars and fifty-six cents all night. Almost not worth keeping the place open I say.

"Ok, Arnold. I will tell him. You get home and get some well deserved sleep. I'll see you in about twelve hours."

"Please don't remind me. Those twelve hours will get here quickly until I get back here and then the freaking clock will slow to a crawl," said Arnold.

"Ha, ha, old man, it started crawling as soon as I got here. By the way...you left a pint of gin under the counter yesterday. Please don't do that again. Unless you want to feel the wrath of old man Sanford."

"Not afraid of him son but I will be careful in the future. He would probably just keep it for himself, ha ha. Here's your first customer, see you later...

Rich observed the short Negro woman struggle to get out of her brand new Mustang. At first she appeared to be in her early sixties but maybe she wasn't that old. The dress she wore was very unusual for these times. She looked as if she had stepped out of a scene from "Gone With The Wind". The perfume she wore was definitely honey suckles and her converse sneakers were an odd contrast with her ruffled dress.

"Good morning. What can I do for you on this fine morning?" said Rich.

"Hello young man. My name is Sandra. I was hoping you could tell me how to get to Copiague, New York. I'm trying to surprise my brother."

"Copiague, New York? I'm sorry but that name doesn't sound familiar. We have some maps inside; they are only a buck."

"Shit son, I can't afford to spend a whole dollar on a map. Back in the old days, the gas attendants always knew how to give directions."

'Ha, ha, maybe they don't make us like they use to. I won't charge you for the map but you can't tell my boss that I gave it to you. Do we have a deal?"

"Deal...can I use your bathroom?"

"Sure, it's right this way."

"Oh my goodness! This place is filthy! I can't use that thing."

"Is something wrong?" said Rich.

"Damn son! You can't give directions. You don't know how to keep your bathroom clean. Just what the heck do you know how to do?"

"What's wrong with the bathroom? No one has ever complained about it before."

"What's wrong with it?

See...that's what I'm always telling my sisters about New Yorkers. The place is filthy... that's what's wrong with it. Do you have a McDonalds nearby? I don't eat their food but they do have clean bathrooms."

"Yes, there is one about a quarter of a mile in that direction."

"Well thank you kindly and have a good day," said Sandra.

Rich quickly went into the bathroom and immediately saw what Sandra was talking about. In the corner behind the toilet was a huge rat that had been caught in a trap. It was still fighting for its life. Arnold was the one who insisted on setting the traps but apparently this morning, he had forgotten to check the trap. Aside from that, the bathroom was spotless. Actually, it was the cleanest part of the Gas Station. As Rich disposed of the rat, he wondered why Sandra hadn't screamed when she saw it. The sight of the huge rat twitching like that would have sent most women and some men running from the horrific scene screaming at the top of their lungs.

It was starting to rain…six hours had passed and only one customer had stopped in. Arnold was right…at this pace Mr. Sanford might indeed need to adjust their hours.

It was such a boring day. The darker it got, the harder it was for Rich to stay awake… he glanced at the clock and was relieved to see the clock slowing ticking toward midnight. He glanced out the window and thought he saw something or someone standing by the gas pumps. He was horrified when he recognized the two figures that belonged to Sergeant Malloy and Detective Gray. Their ghostly figures sent chills through his body as they started pumping gas into the gas cans.

Once the cans were full, Gray lit a huge match, dashed the gas onto the building and sat it afire. Rich was trapped; there was no way for him to get out. The ghostly figures stood outside with satisfied looks on their faces. The heat from the fire was so hot that Rich passed out. Seconds later, someone was poking him in the side. The voice sounded familiar…it was Arnold;

yes Arnold had come to save him. Thanks God for once he was on time.

Arnold poked him one more time in the side and yelled.

"Get your ass up son! Old man Sanford is going to fire your ass if he catches you sleeping on the job like this."

Rich was confused, but slowly came to realize that he had been dreaming. Things just didn't make sense. How could Arnold be alive, if he was dreaming about Detective Gray and Sergeant Malloy? They died after Arnold.

After Rich counted the contents of the register, he bid Arnold a goodnight. He slowly walked toward the bus stop, still confused by the dream. Arnold was very much alive...

The bus took about fifteen minutes to get him to his apartment. The fare was only thirty-five cents. There was the customary free paper at his apartment door that the landlord left everyday. Rich looked at the date on the paper and said oh my God...it was the one year anniversary of the night Malloy and Gray had killed themselves at the garage…

About the Author

Rick Naylor currently resides on the East Coast. He is the author of "His Last Drink" and "The Gas Attendant". Due to the huge success of "The Gas Attendant" he has written a sequel to it.

Other completed books are: "The Advernox Project", "The Chester Project" and "The Final Project" which are the three books of the fabulous trilogy thriller, "The BMX Conspiracy".

Rick welcomes you to go online to Amazon.com or www.booksbyricknaylor.com to review and rate his books.

15021899R10233

Made in the USA
Charleston, SC
13 October 2012